"LET'S PARTY!"

Marc and Carl had them trapped in a crossfire. The Highway Warriors were each down on one knee, their Delta HBARs shouldered. In unison, both of the heavy-barreled M-16s spat superstabilized SS109 full metal–jacketed hornets at the shooters. The lead-core copper-jacketed projectiles spiraled through flesh and sent a misty sea of blood spraying into the air in their wake. The shooters fell to the blood-soaked pavement almost in sequence as Marc and Carl cleansed the lot with sanitizing hellfire.

Another wave of shooters emerged from the burning building. Carl picked the one nearest him and sent a staccato of death singing an eternal death chant into the man's chest. The shooter stopped all forward motion and fell dead to the hot, scorching pavement.

OVERLOAD
Book
10

MICHIGAN
MADNESS

□ □ □

Bob Ham

BANTAM BOOKS
NEW YORK · TORONTO · LONDON · SYDNEY · AUCKLAND

Any similarity to persons, living or dead, places, businesses, governments, governmental entities, organizations, or situations, in existence or having existed, is purely coincidental.

MICHIGAN MADNESS

A Bantam Falcon Book / April 1991

FALCON and the portrayal of a boxed "f" are trademarks of Bantam Books, a division of Bantam Doubleday Dell Publishing Group, Inc.

ISBN 0-553-28998-5

Published simultaneously in the United States and Canada

Bantam Books are published by Bantam Books, a division of Bantam Doubleday Dell Publishing Group, Inc. Its trademark, consisting of the words "Bantam Books" and the portrayal of a rooster, is Registered in U.S. Patent and Trademark Office and in other countries. Marca Registrada. Bantam Books, 666 Fifth Avenue, New York, New York 10103.

PRINTED IN THE UNITED STATES OF AMERICA

RAD   0 9 8 7 6 5 4 3 2 1

This one's for the Placeways
—Gary, Cheryl, Shane, and Tara—
once neighbors . . . forever friends, who took us
in, treated us like family, and guided us on an
adventure through their native Michigan. The
images will remain forever etched in our minds
and your kindness forever endeared in our hearts.
God Bless

The unleashed power of the atom has changed everything except our ways of thinking. Thus we are drifting toward a catastrophe beyond comparison. We shall require substantially a new manner of thinking if mankind is to survive.

—ALBERT EINSTEIN

There is, in our midst, a power more volatile than the most unstable compound. More lethal than the most advanced warhead. More contagious than the deadliest virus. That power is greed. It is an ugly beast latently dormant in the very nature of mankind. Often stirred by opportunity, the beast rears its ugly head and devours the men who harbor it. And when it preys upon the lives of innocents, I will hunt the beast and destroy him.

—MARC LEE

Chapter One

□ □ □

Tuesday Morning

Something just didn't feel right. Carney Putnam didn't know exactly what it was. He couldn't put his finger on it. But one thing he did know—the fog and the cool breeze drifting across Lake Michigan left him with an eerie sensation. There was something about it he couldn't explain, but his gut instincts were screaming at him and telling him to step up the caution level. Even if just a little.

He'd spent thirty-five years running cargo across the broad expanse of water, and he knew when things didn't feel the way they were supposed to. Maybe it was because he was always worried when he carried plutoniun for the government.

And this was one of those nights.

The old tub, the *Polly P,* creaked and groaned as she plowed north against a head wind on the giant open body of freshwater. The diesel engines below hummed a dull, boring tune as they sent the power to turn the twin screws beneath the water. The repetitious clanking of the cams and the hum of the radar antenna rotating overhead at the bridge were sufficiently monotonous to cause even an energetic man to go to sleep.

1

At three in the morning, Carney felt anything but energetic. Right now, he wanted to go below to his modest captain's quarters, sip a glass of brandy, kick his boots off, smoke a stogie, and relax in his bunk until the waves against the bow caused him to drift off into restful sleep.

But there could be no sleep tonight. Not with three of his regular ten-man crew out with some gut-wrenching viral infection. There was too much to do and too few hands to get it done. The three replacements he had hustled from a bar on the docks at Milwaukee were working out okay, but they didn't know the ropes. By the time they learned to do things the way he liked them done, the regulars would be back. Hopefully, at least.

Gurley Galopagus opened the rickety door to the bridge and walked in. "Mornin', Cap'n. A damn-sight bone-chilling out there this morn'n, hey?"

"Aye, Gurley. I was just thinking to myself that this night ain't feelin' quite right. Maybe it's the fog. Fog does that to you, you know," Putnam said. "I recall once on a troop transport ship back during the big war we got ourselves swallowed up in the fog. It'll have you barking up your own ass before you know it."

Gurley laughed. "Aye, Cap'n, maybe that's it. Maybe the fog has us all chasin' our tails. What's weather like ahead?"

"Clearing by mornin', winds out of the north at fifteen knots. More of that arctic blast headed our way. Get's nippy when the north wind blows," Putnam said. He made a slight adjustment in the freighter's course and checked his wheel movement against the compass mounted between him and the forward glass. "Fog doesn't bother me as much as runnin' through these shallows. Even with radar and the depth sounder, it still makes my skin crawl sometimes."

"Can't say I won't welcome it, the northern that is. Maybe it'll blow this fog out of here. I can't figger why the shallows bother you, Cap'n. You've shot 'em a thousand times."

"And it's bothered me a thousand times, Gurley."

"It's a long way to Bay City. Goin' around the point at the peninsula might get a little on the frigid side with the northern blowin' in. Hey, but what the hell, huh? That's why we got them heaters down below. Am I right, Cap'n?"

Putnam laughed. "Right as usual, Gurley."

The rig shook with a resounding vibration, followed an instant later by the roar of an explosion. Almost before the roar died away, the *Polly P* listed hard to starboard, sending the two men crashing to the deck.

When Putnam and Gurley regained their balance, their faces were pale. "What the hell was it, Cap'n?" Gurley yelled.

Blood trickled down Putnam's face. He fought to stand and held tightly to the wheel. He looked aft and saw towers of black smoke funneling toward the sky. "Damage report, Gurley. Get us a damage report. We've blown somewhere. Intercom's dead."

Gurley forced himself to walk against the list and moved toward the door.

It swung open, and a man dressed in solid black stood there, his face cold and brutal. In his hands there was a .45 automatic. "Not a good night to be out of doors, mate."

Gurley froze.

Putnam looked through weakening eyes at the figure holding the gun. "What the hell is this?"

"Deep six," the man answered. He lifted the .45 on line and fired three shots into Gurley's face.

Gurley jerked backwards as blood splayed in the air and filled the cabin with crimson-red death.

Putnam leapt for the window, but three more messengers of death flew from the bore of the smoking .45. They tore through his flesh like starving barracudas shooting through a school of shad. And when their energy was spent, Putnam's life drifted away into the dark fog and left him lying in a drifting sea of blood.

The *Polly P* rolled hard to port now, and her stern swallowed up the water of the great lake. Another explosion vibrated through her dying carcass. In minutes, her bow lifted out of the water, and she sank to the dark sandy bottom below.

Wednesday Morning

Marc Lee crouched in the scrubby underbrush and scanned the trucking terminal with his rubber-armored binoculars. He could see them in the light of the mercury-vapor lights, men in camouflaged field dress, milling around all three buildings within the fenced compound below. He spoke softly into the throat microphone of the tactical radio harness connected to his Icom U-16 transceiver. "I count eighteen men and seven rigs. How's the total from your angle."

Carl Browne spoke softly also. He crouched in the darkness a hundred yards west of Marc and watched the movement in the compound. "I got the same count. We do it by the numbers?"

"Is there any other way?" Marc asked. He knew before he said it that his partner would have called the play the same way he did. The Delta Force Warriors turned Highway Warriors had been together far too long for it to go any other way. It had started in military basic training. There a camaraderie had grown that had lasted through service in Delta Force and on to the present in what had become a never-ending war. But this war, unlike the ones they had known before, was fought on the soil of the very country they were fighting to preserve.

Carl made a touch-check of his arms and accessories.

The Beretta 92-F 9mm was snug in the shoulder leather under his left arm. The Smith & Wesson 5906 9mm rode comfortably on his hip in the Uncle Mike's nylon rig. He slid the Smith from its sheath and checked the magazine. He knew it was full, but it was a practice he had developed many years ago, an evolution of field-honed survival strategies etched in his mind from the bloody battles of a world gone mad.

Satisfied with the Smith, Carl checked the Beretta. With the hammer-drops thumbed up on both auto pistols, they were ready for instant duty. That done, he dropped the thirty-round magazine from the Colt Delta HBAR M-16/A2 5.56mm full-auto assault rifle. He pressed the top round of SS109 ammo to be sure the stick was full. It was. He shoved the Colt aluminum mag back into the well, slapped it home, and heard the familiar reassuring click. Then he pulled the charging lever all the way to the rear and let it slam closed, taking with it the first round from the top of the thirty-rounder.

He slid the sound-suppressed 9mm Uzi from his shoulder, dropped the stick from its well, and made the obligatory mag check. Then he slid the little subgun back on his shoulder sling. An experimentally modified LAW disposable rocket-launcher tube was also strung across his back on a sling. He carried the fragmentation projectiles for the tube in his oversized fanny pack. A couple of CS gas grenades and a half-dozen fragmentation grenades completed his belt arsenal. His trusted Parker-Imai K-632 fighting knife rode low on his left hip.

Marc made his own weapons check. He too carried a Colt Delta HBAR M-16/A2 in 5.56mm and sound-suppressed Uzi chambered for 9mm Parabellum. But rather than a LAW tube, he carried an experimental laser sighting device similar in size to an old .30 caliber M-1 Carbine. The little Zytel-stocked fieldpiece shot a beam of invisible light up to one thousand yards. The beam itself was harmless, but it paved the way to awesome destruction of the laser-guided missiles Carl carried in addition to the frag rounds for the LAW. Carl's tube had been modified for feed-fire with the fiberglass high-tech guided explosive. When the laser sight fell on the target, Carl could finger a lightning-fast missile. The new explosive round was designated DFEP-Hellfire, for Delta Force experimental portable-hellfire class.

The trucking terminal inside the security fence below them was a front. The men in camos weren't truckers either. They were a cell of highly trained renegade gunmen bound for the disruption of normal civilization. American terrorists. Guns for hire to the highest bidder—damn the cause and to hell with the reason. They were misguided souls who had made the wrong choices for their lives. And now those choices were about to cause collection of the ultimate debt. Cleansing fire sat just 150 yards away cradled in the arms of Marc Lee and Carl Browne. The mighty talons of justice were ready to swoop down and pluck the savages from the very society they threatened.

Marc finished his weapons check and lifted the binoculars to his face for one more satisfying look before he sent scorching hellfire to where the evildoers stood. He spoke into the VOX microphone unit once more. "Five seconds on my mark, Major. Five, four, three, two, one. Let's party!"

Carl was up and running with the count. He moved forward in a crouch, the Delta HBAR poised in his hands and ready to breathe death. He kept his eyes fixed on the area where the men in camo fatigues moved around, oblivious to the attack. Carl glanced only once to his right, into the darkness where he knew Marc would be moving also. He caressed the HBAR's trigger like a mother clinging to her newborn baby. It took twenty seconds for him to reach the outer security fence. Then he stopped, removed a pair of heavy bolt cutters from his musette bag, and clipped a hole in the diamond-patterned fencing. That done, he dropped the cutters back into the pack, slid the LAW tube from his back, and dropped to his knees.

Marc was five seconds behind Carl. He worked around to the east until he reached the area he had chosen for his entry into the compound. Like Carl, he clipped a hole in the fencing, peeled back the heavy wire, and slid the carbine-style electronic sight from his shoulder. He chose the larger of the three buildings and aimed the laser into a huge overhead garage door. He spoke through the VOX unit attached to his transceiver. "Beacon's burning. Give 'em Hellfire."

Carl slid a fiberglass rocket into the tube until it touched home. He aimed in the direction of the huge door, saw the digital lock appear on the electronic sight, and touched off the missile. A resounding *whoosh* echoed through the night. The experimental Hellfire-style missile shot from the tube and streaked across the night. Midway between the fence and the tube, the rocket corrected its course and homed in on the invisible laser beam poised on the building door.

In the time it took the camo-clad men to react to the whoosh, the experimental rocket made contact. The early-morning sky lit bright from the intensity of the explosion. An orange fireball shot skyward. The concussion from the explosion rolled across the paved lot like a cyclonic whirl-wind, knocking the camo men to the ground before they could move.

Marc slung the laser-sight device over his shoulder and moved at the sound of the explosion. Heat from the intense fire seared the pavement, but Marc zigzagged across the lot. He held the Delta HBAR by the pistol grip with his right hand. His index finger was threaded through the trigger guard and ready to fire at the blink of an eye.

Carl slung the tube over his shoulder and moved out also. He ran across the lot and stopped in the cover of one of the buildings adjacent to the one now burning uncontrollably. He dropped to one knee and shouldered the Delta HBAR. He leveled the sight on one of the men who was struggling to get up from the ground and unsheathe an automatic pistol from a holster on his hip. Carl let the guy clear leather and search the fence line with the weapon. When the pistol-wielding man finally stood, Carl tapped out a three-round burst of sizzling death.

The shooter took all three rounds in the chest and pivoted back to the ground. Other men scrambled to their feet now, drawing weapons as they scurried for cover. Carl laid the sights on another one and tapped off his second three-round burst. The shooter took the hits in the neck and spiraled backward into dark eternity.

Shots were coming from inside the building nearest Marc on the opposite side of the burning building. Shooters fired into the darkness without a target. Sound shots. The lot and the buildings were consumed with fire and chaos now. Men were moving erratically and searching for cover from the unseen menace descending upon them from the darkness.

Marc found two men crouched behind a line of fifty-five gallon barrels. He watched them for a minute while they searched the opposite end of the lot for the source of the hellstorm. He strained hard to read the white labeling on the barrels. It was difficult, but he finally read VARSOL. "Bingo," he mumbled. He reached to his utility belt and retrieved a hand grenade. He held the spoon tightly against the body and pulled the pin free. Then he tossed the grenade with pinpoint precision between the wall of the building and the barrels.

The men jerked around and searched the darkness for the source of the loud cracking thud emitted when the grenade struck the pavement. By the time they found it, it was too late. He heard one man yell "Grenade" an instant before the pineapple exploded. The guy's frantic cry was lost in the shattering explosion when the fire from the grenade ignited the barrels of Varsol. The ground shook, and more fire joined the towers of smoke already belching from the burning building. The explosion lifted the men from the ground and sent them sailing into the air. Their flight ended when their flaming, lifeless torsos slapped into the pavement and rolled to a stop.

Men ran from the other two buildings now, their weapons chattering a full-auto death chant into targets hidden in the darkness.

Marc and Carl had them trapped in a cross fire. The Highway Warriors were both down on one knee, their Delta HBARs shouldered. In unison, both of the heavy-barreled M-16s spat superstabilized SS109 metal-jacketed hornets at the shooters. The lead-core projectiles spiraled through flesh and sent a misty sea of blood spraying into the air in their wake. The shooters fell to the blood-soaked pavement as Marc and Carl cleansed the lot with hellfire.

Another wave of shooters emerged from the burning building and the one nearest Carl. Every man who came into view was firing wildly. Carl picked the one nearest him and sent a staccato burst of death into the man's chest. The shooter fell dead to the scorching pavement.

Marc saw three men running across the lot toward one of the eighteen-wheelers parked in the shadows at the opposite side of the lot. He trained the sight of the Delta HBAR on them and popped a burst of 5.56mm justice. The shooters took the hits before they could move another step.

The fire had spread to the building nearest Marc with the assistance of the exploded Varsol petroleum cleaning solvent. There were screams of confusion from inside. And behind it, the roar of a diesel engine starting caught Marc's attention. He spoke into the microphone. "We got a rabbit out back. When he clears the building, I'll drop the dot on him and see if you can send a bird up his ass."

"Roger," Carl replied. He laid the Delta HBAR across his lap and grabbed for the DFEP tube. He shuffled around and retrieved a rocket from the fanny pack, slid it into the tube, and cradled the trigger. "I'm ready, Colonel."

The fleeing eighteen-wheeler appeared at the corner of the building and sped across the lot toward the locked gates at the end opposite Marc. Marc laid the invisible sight on the fuel tanks. "Now!" he said into the throat mike.

Carl aimed in the general direction of the truck and touched the firing trigger. Another whoosh spat from the tube and sent a roaring thunderbolt toward the fleeing rig. The electronic homing device on the nose of the fiberglass projectile found the source it sought and crashed into the rig's fuel tanks with an earth-shattering explosion. The rig listed to one side, rocked hard, and burst into fiery fragments amid a scorching cataclysmic fireball.

"Good shootin', Major," Marc said. "You sure took the wind out of his sails. Let's move in on 'em and mop this up."

"Affirmative," Carl replied. He slung the tube over his shoulder and cradled the Delta HBAR. He moved forward against a hailstorm of bullets that sailed erratically into the darkness. He ran a zigzag pattern, and the mighty A2 sent swarms of killer hornets into the remaining hardcases.

Marc did the same thing. He was up and running into the lighted area of the lot before the trapped men spotted him. He screamed at them, "Drop your weapons and lie on the pavement."

His command was met with automatic weaponfire when the camo-clad hardcases spun around. Marc dropped prone and spent the remainder of his thirty-round magazine into them. There wasn't time to get to another stick. He drew his Smith & Wesson 5906 from his hip holster and fired the first round double-action into the shooter who carried an Ingram MAC-10. The first round struck the man in the upper chest, and then two more semiauto shots tore through his midsection. The shooter flung the Ingram wildly and twisted to the pavement like a tumbling corkscrew.

Marc grabbed another thirty-round stick from his musette bag and slapped it up the well of the HBAR. He pressed the bolt release, and the heavy spring slapped the bolt shut while it stripped the first round from the top of the stick. He moved out now, all the visible shooters down. He went to the building nearest him and kicked the door open. He swept the inside with the muzzle of the HBAR and found nothing. He moved through the building carefully, checking each small room and doorway before he entered. Then he reached the warehouse section and kicked another door open. Smoke belched out at him, followed immediately by heavy gunfire from a pair of hidden shooters. Marc returned a short burst of autofire and lifted a fragmentation grenade from his belt. He jerked the pin free and tossed the handbomb in the direction of the gunfire. Then he ducked out into the hallway and hit the floor. A loud explosion preceded agonized screams as the two shooters met eternity. Marc rushed into the warehouse room and searched for survivors. He found none.

Carl entered the building he had used seconds earlier for cover. He searched for targets with the sweeping barrel of the HBAR, but there were none visible. He did a room-by-room search. He reached a barricaded room near the back with a heavy open lock dangling from the door. He moved the door open slowly and fired a burst into the room.

There was no reply.

Carl rushed into the room and stopped cold. There on the floor lay the brutalized body of their inside man, Bernie Compton, silent and dead. Beside Compton's body were a dozen empty wooden crates with distinct military markings and encodes. Carl spoke into the microphone. "I got Compton and the goods," he said.

"Roger. It's clean over on this end. Where are you?"

"First building on the end. You comin'?"

"Yeah," Marc replied. "On my way. How's Compton?"

"Stone-cold dead," Carl replied. "All the crates are empty too."

"Wonderful," Marc replied. In seconds he had worked his way to the building where Carl stood staring at Compton's brutalized body.

"Nice touch, huh?" Carl said as he stared at Compton's lifeless form. The guy's throat was slit from ear to ear, and his tongue protruded through the opening and dangled from the place where his Adam's apple should have been. "A damned Colombian necktie. These people are barbarians."

"Yeah," Marc replied as he felt his stomach churning. "And the hell of it is, they've got a dozen experimental low-yield personal nuclear rocket tubes. And God only knows how much ammo they've pilfered to go with it."

"Yeah," Carl said. "Compton gave his life to get these bastards, and look at him now. We've got to find Tommy Dominick before they find out how to make more missiles for these things."

"All they need is plutonium and some ingenuity, and we've got a serious problem on our hands," Marc replied. "Tommy Dominick's middle name is crazy. Compton is evidence to that."

Carl nodded. Both Warriors spun around in unison when they heard footsteps coming behind them.

Chapter Two

□ □ □

Andy Starr steered the eighteen-foot pleasure boat toward the shore at the north end of the Dunes, near Silver Lake State Park on the eastern shore of Lake Michigan. Rick Hosfelt sat in the bow seat and watched as the boat's nose slid across the sandy bottom of the lake and stopped against the shore. He jumped out and landed in wet sand, a rope in his hand to secure the boat. He found a large rock and tied the rope off.

Starr secured the engine, made his way to the bow, and jumped ashore. He immediately stripped his wet suit, dried himself off with a towel, and fumbled through a duffel bag for dry clothes. When he was finished, he grabbed the line securing the boat and nodded to Hosfelt. "Give me a hand and let's pull this thing up on the shore about five feet."

Hosfelt grabbed the rope and pulled. "You ready to unload the wares?" he asked.

"Soon as we move to the top of the hill and give the signal. You go do that, and I'll make a fast check of the weapons," Starr replied.

"Got it," Hosfelt said. He lifted a nylon carrypack from the bow and disappeared into the darkness toward the mammoth sand dunes.

Starr retrieved a small flashlight from his duffel bag and switched it on. He found a black nylon totebag, lifted it to the shore, and unzipped it. Inside were a dozen brick-size, off-white plastique explosive charges. Each charge of Composition-4 had a small digital-clock display mounted on the top and secured into it. Starr removed one from the bag. He checked the digital timer and climbed into the boat. When he had worked his way to the rear, he positioned the firm plastique against the fuel tanks and pressed the brick into place. Then he set the digital timer to fifteen minutes and pressed the *start* switch on the clock.

Beyond the shore in the darkness, Hosfelt struggled to climb the steep face of the high sand dune. Each step buried his feet deep in the shifting sand. The struggle took several minutes, but he finally reached the top. He sat on the edge of the crest and prowled through the nylon carrypack. When he found the transmitter, he lifted it from the bag and switched it on. He extended the telescopic antenna and flipped the subminiature *transmit* switch to activate the tone signal. Hosfelt left the transmitter on for a full minute before he switched it off and collapsed the antenna. That done, he laid the tone transmitter back into the carrypack and retrieved his handheld radio transceiver. He switched it on and waited for the call.

Starr, meanwhile, moved quickly to unload everything he wanted from the boat. He carried a half-dozen nylon packs to the bow and stashed them safely on the shore. After five minutes, all that remained were the heavy-metal waterproof containers of plutonium stolen from the *Polly P*.

Hosfelt walked back alongside Starr. "Three to five minutes."

"Good," Starr replied. "Let's get these cases unloaded, and we'll be ready to shove out when the buggy gets here."

Hosfelt and Starr climbed across the bow of the boat and moved toward the three crate-size, heavy-metal cases.

Each case was painted bright yellow with the international symbol for radioactive materials painted on the side. Heavy-duty carrying handles protruded from each case on the sides near the top. Starr and Hosfelt each fisted a handle and lifted the first case. They strained under the weight but managed to move the airtight, water-proof case forward toward the bow. They sat it on the bow seat, and Hosfelt jumped from the boat into the sand. He lifted while Starr nudged the case to the lip of the bow. Then Starr jumped out of the boat, and the men moved the heavy case to the area on the shore where their gear was stowed.

"Those things sure are heavy," Hosfelt said.

"Most of it is packaging," Starr replied. "There's ten pounds of plutonium in each case. The other eighty or ninety pounds is packaging."

"The water didn't damage it?" Hosfelt asked.

"No," Starr replied. "When I blew the freighter and the materials sank, these containers kept this stuff safe and dry. It could stay in one of these cases for a hundred years and never change states."

"How long you figure before somebody finds the *Polly P*?" Hosfelt asked.

"With weather like it is and the trip around the peninsula as slow as it is for a freighter, it could take a day or two. My guess is nobody even knows she's missing yet. As soon as they decide something isn't right, there'll be a major search. Feds get real excited when they think there's dangerous cargo missing. By the time they find her and realize the stuff is gone, we'll have it safely stashed where we can get to it and move it at our leisure."

Hosfelt shrugged his shoulders and climbed over the bow of the boat.

Starr was directly behind him. "Let's step on it. The timers are in place and counting." He glanced at the illuminated dial of his wristwatch. "Nine minutes left."

Hosfelt reached another container and grabbed the handle. They moved the case to the shore beside the first one. It took two and a half minutes to unload both crates.

Starr took a deep breath and moved to the towline securing the boat. He untied it and tossed it into the boat. "Give me a hand, and let's shove this little tool back into the water."

Hosfelt obliged and they shoved the boat back into the cool waters of Lake Michigan.

Starr climbed aboard and fired the engine. He backed the boat into the water until he could spin it around facing westward into the giant lake. The inboard-outboard power plant rumbled and sputtered. Starr tilted the engine down until it was canted properly for a trimmed-out high-speed run. He tied the steering wheel firmly in place and eased the boat back until he was in knee-deep water. Then he climbed from the back of the boat and jumped ashore. "Hit it," he said.

Hosfelt moved a small joystick lever on a control box he had retrieved from one of the nylon packs. The unit resembled a large model-airplane radio control panel. A long telescopic antenna protruded from the top, and four joystick levers were situated on the face of the control. At the electronic command, the boat shifted into gear and moved slowly across the dark water. Hosfelt let it get a hundred feet from the shore and opened the throttle. The boat's bow shot out of the water as the stern squatted. The engine roared, and the high-powered pleasure craft disappeared into the morning darkness.

Starr grinned. "About the time she clears the horizon, best I can calculate. What do you think?"

"That sounds about right," Hosfelt agreed. He turned when he heard the muffled sound of a dune buggy approaching from behind.

The buggy reached Starr and Hosfelt, and rolled to a

gentle stop. Two men were barely visible in the open cab. They wore helmets equipped with night-vision infrared optics. The men stripped the helmets and laid them in the seats as they climbed from the machine. "Well, boss, you're right on time," said the man on the passenger's side.

"Always, Bowman," Starr replied. "Help us load this stuff, and we're out of here."

The men moved quickly. In three minutes, the metal cases were loaded into the buggy and rolling toward the top of the first high sand dune east of the shore.

Starr looked down at the illuminated face of his wristwatch as the dune buggy sped through the darkness over the treacherous surface of the massive dunes. He could see nothing except the watch, but he knew Bowman and Warner could see everything through the night-vision helmets. His watch showed fifteen seconds. Starr twisted around in his seat and watched the horizon behind him. Exactly fifteen seconds later, a bright flash appeared on the horizon and immediately vanished.

Starr turned back around and enjoyed the ride.

Marc and Carl crouched low behind the cover of the empty crates. The sound drew closer, but no one appeared.

They waited. Each Highway Warrior sat with his index finger cradling the trigger of the Colt Delta HBAR, his eyes searching the opening in the doorway.

Footsteps moved toward the door.

"Artie, are you sure they're in this building?" a voice asked from somewhere outside the door.

"I know I saw two men come in here, Lou. Maybe they went out the back," Artie said.

"Suits the hell outta me," Lou said. "Ben and T.J. can deal with 'em. Let's give it the once-over, and if we don't see anything, we're out of this place. If you saw two come in here; there must be more out there in the darkness around the fence line. I'm for haulin' ass before they really hit this place. What say?"

"Maybe we ought to check in the storage room. Dominick kept the snitch in there before he snuffed him," Artie said. "If they ain't in here, I'm ready to book it."

"I can dig it," Lou replied. He moved toward the doorway and stopped at the threshold. "It's dark as pitch in there. I can't see anything."

"Hell, Lou. They ain't in there. If they were, they'd have shot your ass off," Artie replied.

"Yeah, you're right," Lou said. "Let's get one of the trucks and leave."

Lou turned to leave and Artie followed.

Marc saw the chance to take both of the rent-a-slime thugs. "Hey, Lou. Artie was wrong!" he yelled.

Lou spun around first. The muzzle of his subgun spat streaks of deadly fire. The pellets perforated the wall above Marc's and Carl's heads. Chips of drywall and wood splintered and fragmented across the room.

Marc tapped out a triple three-round burst from his 5.56mm HBAR. Hot brass pelted the concrete floor as his sizzlers tore through the doorway.

Lou was on the floor now, Artie beside him. Both fired their subguns into the darkness of the storage room. White-orange tongues of flames spat from their muzzles. Lou and Artie scrambled for some kind of cover that would allow them a line of fire. Lou touched off another subgun burst. The searing 9mm Parabellums chewed through more drywall on the back wall of the room and created another hailstorm of debris throughout the room.

Marc leaned against Carl and whispered. "Feed 'em some pineapple, Major," he said.

Carl kept his right index finger on the HBAR's trigger and his eyes fixed on the location of the last muzzle flash from the assaulting shooters. He made a grab with his left hand toward the utility belt around his waist. He slipped a fragmentation grenade free of the retainer, moved the high explosive to his face, and clamped down on the safety pin with his teeth with true Hollywood heroics. It was a move he knew seldom occurred in real life, one that presented an excellent opportunity to lose some teeth, but the current situation demanded improvisation. He held the spoon firmly against the hard steel body and nudged the pineapple forward slowly until the safety pin slid free. He moved his arm back into a solid throwing position and waited patiently.

The wait wasn't long. Another burst of lead sailed into the room. Even before it stopped riveting the walls and empty crates, Carl tossed the frag pineapple toward the doorway. It landed with a solid metallic thud and bounced across the floor.

"Grenade, Artie!" Lou yelled. He scrambled to get to his feet.

Artie was already up and running at the sound of the thud for the doorway at the back of the building, but Lou couldn't move fast enough. He wasted precious milliseconds searching the darkness for the handbomb.

Then he found it, at the precise instant it exploded in his face. Searing, jagged shards of steel shrapnel cut through him like flying steak knives. His last sound in life was a breath-filled sigh when the scorching metal chewed through his lungs and forced the air from them. Shattered bone fragments and chunks of bloody flesh sailed through the night and coated the walls of the hallway. A gaping hole appeared in his upper chest and neck as the remains of his body slammed into the wall behind him. The ravaged torso slid slowly to the floor and settled in a quickly growing pool of warm blood.

Artie didn't move fast enough either. The deadly rain of fragmented steel descended on him like a runaway buzz saw. The lethal shards ripped through his legs and cut the femoral arteries. Blood spurted through the holes in his tattered pants with every beat of his terrified heart. He hit the door at the back of the building and collapsed through it onto the pavement. He felt his life seep from him one heartbeat at a time. Through the terror that ate at his mind, he realized he had dropped his subgun when he fell through the door. He saw it in the glow of a mercury-vapor lamp at the end of the compound lot. It lay just half an arm's length away, pointed at the doorway through which he had fallen. As he leaned forward to get it, the door burst open, and the massive silhouette of a man appeared. He couldn't see the man's face, but he knew it was one of the men from the dark room. What he could see was the muzzle of an awesome weapon pointed at his face.

"No, no, no!" Marc said. He stood with the barrel of a Grizzly .45 Magnum rock-steady and pointed at Artie. Marc was in the shadows and the barrel of the weapon protruded into the light. Marc's voice was deathly cold, his words even and firm. "I see it in your eyes. You're wondering, 'Will he shoot me?' Well, there's only one way you'll ever know. Just keep moving your hand toward that gun. All you have to do is search your soul for the answer to one simple question: Were you born brain-dead, or do I make you that way?"

Artie froze, his hand only a few inches from the trigger housing of the subgun. He could see the unyielding barrel of the giant pistol. "Who are you?"

"I'm a collection agent. I work for society."

Artie still didn't move. He felt his heart weakening as more precious blood spurted to the pavement in an ever-growing puddle. "What do you want?"

Marc snickered. "Oh, it's simple, really. I want some answers . . . or your life. It's entirely up to you."

"What answers?" Artie asked weakly, his right hand quivering near the subgun.

"Where are the PNDs and Tommy Dominick?"

Artie struggled for breath, his strength and his sight growing weaker with every frantic beat of his heart. "Dominick took the PNDs. I don't know where he went. Owosso? Maybe the Dunes. I swear I don't know. He was gonna give us a new assignment tomorrow night. I swear it, mister. "

"What's he planning to do with the PNDs?"

"Sell 'em. Use 'em. Hell, I don't know," Artie said pleadingly. "You gonna kill me?"

Marc laughed a sarcastic laugh. "I think you were born brain-dead. Killing you would be a waste of a perfectly good bullet. I think I'll just let you bleed to death. That's what leeches like you like, isn't it? Bleeding society to death one wound at a time? Tell me, was it worth it?"

Artie breathed hard and fast, and lunged for the subgun in a move of fatal desperation.

He was far too slow.

Marc tapped the trigger, and the Grizzly roared. A 260-grain Speer hollowpoint spun from the barrel at 1,580 feet per second amid a brilliant flash of fire and gunsmoke. The copper-jacketed agent of death bored through Artie's forehead directly between his eyes. His eyes bulged forward, and his head opened up like an overripe tomato as his body jackknifed backward. His legs bent at an awkward angle under the twisting surge of his body. His muscles twitched spasmodically for a few seconds before they relaxed forever.

"Now you're permanently brain-dead, rent-a-slime," Marc growled as he lowered the Grizzly, thumbed down the hammer, and shoved it back into its waistline holster at the small of his back.

There was gunfire on the other side of the building

now. Carl. And from the sound, the firefight had rekindled. Marc spun around to his right. He surveyed the shadows and moved stealthily toward them. He hugged the back wall of the building as he moved to the end opposite where he and Carl had entered. He crouched low, the Colt Delta HBAR ready to erase anything in its path.

He saw a man running toward the end of the building from the area in the rear where the remaining eighteen-wheelers were parked. Marc let him go until he could reach the corner of the building where the man disappeared. He moved carefully to the corner and eased his head around.

He saw him—a shooter crouched on one knee ready to send death toward Carl's position.

Marc fell prone and stretched around the corner. He unleashed a full-auto burst of SS109 copper-sheathed lightning. The pellets found the shooter and chewed his life from him before he could react.

Marc took a quick recon look and jumped to his feet. He ran hard, the shadows of the building his only cover. He reached the edge of the building and dropped low to look around that corner.

More shooters. Three.

Marc lifted a grenade from his belt and yanked the safety pin free. He tossed the pineapple toward them and fell low, covering his ears as he sought cover.

The grenade exploded and the shooters flew wildly into the air.

The gunfire stopped.

"Let's mop it up and take it home," Marc said into the Tact headgear.

"Nothin' movin' this way, Colonel. Wanna get the charges in place and hit it?"

"Affirmative," Marc replied. "We've been here too long. Company has got to be coming."

"I need two minutes, and I'll leave this place so the guy that built it won't even recognize it," Carl said.

"Do it. I'll cover for you."

Carl moved to place the specially formulated DFC-2 charges around strategic areas of the compound. He set the timers and moved toward the fence. "I'm rollin', Colonel."

"Go!" Marc replied. "I'm behind you."

"Roger."

Marc moved toward the fence when he saw Carl disappear through the hole cut earlier. He reached his exit and crawled through. He ran hard and caught up with Carl at the appointed position two hundred yards from the compound.

The earth beneath their feet trembled and vibrated when the world within the fenced compound erupted into a massive ball of flame. Marc paused and glanced back at the leaping tongues of cleansing fire. "Now we have to find Tommy Dominick. Something tells me he is going to be a very unhappy fugitive."

"Yeah," Carl said. "But Dominick ain't gonna be nearly as unhappy as the Boss if somebody uses those PNDs."

Chapter Three

□ □ □

Wednesday Afternoon

The sun glistened off choppy whitecaps rolling across the broad expanse of Lake Michigan roughly between Milwaukee, Wisconsin, and Muskegon, Michigan. The prevailing wind came out of the north with a frigid ferocity uncommon for midsummer in central Michigan. The hard arctic low-pressure system had dipped deep into the central United States as far south as Tennessee. With it came record-low summer temperatures.

As the sun peaked over the great natural mounds of the Dunes on Lake Michigan's eastern shore, it shone like a mirror across the crystal-clear waters of Silver Lake. A few adventurous boaters sped across the dying inland lake, oblivious to the chilling mist propelled skyward by their speeding boats. On the tranquil shores of Silver Lake in a rented cabin, Tommy Dominick watched the sands of the Dunes shift in the wind. Like stinging needles, the tiny particles sailed through the air to further the impending death of Silver Lake. As he puffed on an imported cigar, Dominick theorized he could come back in ten years to the place where he now stood, and the cabin, like other cabins before it, would be buried beneath tons of shifted sand a hundred feet high. And with the burial of the cabin beneath the shifting sands, another five or ten feet of the gorgeously scenic Silver Lake would be lost to the uncontrollable forces of nature.

Dominick turned from the scenic view of nature's work and walked inside from the wooden deck. He stuffed the cigar into an ashtray on the coffee table beside the sofa, sat down, then picked up a computer printout, and thumbed through it. After three or four minutes of digesting the information, he looked up at the hard, lean face of Andy Starr. "Any word on extended security for tonight's move of the PND projectiles?"

Starr dropped the issue of *Soldier of Fortune* onto his lap and looked into Dominick's dark eyes. "Nothing from recon. We'll have it before the day is out. The move shouldn't take place until sometime after midnight. Since the escapade at the terminal—and if they know the boat is missing—you can bet your hairy ass the government will pull out all of the stops. They know we have the tubes, and they know we have some of the projectiles. Any other projectiles will be guarded like the gates of Fort Knox."

"And we have that covered, do we not?" Dominick asked.

"Of course. If they move 'em, we can take them out whenever and wherever we want. They won't know what hit them," Starr said confidently.

"*What*, I can handle. It's *who* that still makes me nervous. We will be able to command great attention and respect if we have the remainder of those PNDs. If we mess up, any of our people, then we die or end up with real hard time," Dominick said.

"Don't sweat it, Tommy," Starr said. "I told you I'd take care of the boat and the plutonium, and I did. Right? This thing tonight will be a piece of cake. There's a dozen small towns and a thousand places in the boonies where this convoy will have to roll tonight. My strategies are well planned and immaculately executed. Throughout my extensive career, I have never failed on a mission. That's why I'm still here, and that's why you hired me. I see no reason to start screwing up now. Do you?"

Dominick nodded and reached for the cigar. He pulled a disposable butane lighter from his pocket and relit the stogie. "These people from across the big pond get real excited when a delivery isn't made on time. We don't get the goods there, and they'll flip-flop to the Russians in a New York minute. And something you should remember, Andy. These guys do a flip-flop, they ain't real keen on leaving any witnesses around. That means we got big-time problems. You catch my drift?"

Starr's face hardened. "Camel jockeys. Who gives a shit? Ten of them ain't serious competition for one of my men. I got the best. The very best there is. Period. They want to play hard games, I got the people to do it. They get too brazen with me, and I'll nuke 'em with a sample of the goods. I don't trust the bastards, and I damn sure don't like 'em."

"Right. Is that why seventeen of your 'best' were chopped down like ripe sunflowers last night?"

Starr sat, speechless, but his face reflected total disgust at the comment.

"Caution, Andy. Overconfidence can be fatal."

"Yes, Tommy, and fatalism can be fatal also," Starr said. "My men will find whoever is responsible for the melee at the trucking terminal last night. When they do, the perpetrators will die a death far worse than any they could imagine in their most horrible nightmares. But now it's first things first."

Tommy Dominick stood from the sofa and walked back to the sliding glass doors at the deck overlooking Silver Lake. He took a deep puff off the cigar and let the heavy smoke settle into his lungs. "If it was the feds or military intelligence, we might have a serious problem. There's little question the plutonium and the salvaged PNDs will be safe in the dunes. Before tomorrow, it will be buried under a couple of feet of shifting sand. It's off the beaten path, and this is the last place on the face of this earth anyone would ever look. We need to get the other PNDs and store them also. But you must beware of futile retribution, Andy. Sometimes it's just best to cut your losses and let it go."

Starr's voice grew deep, firm, and low. "Tommy, you obviously don't understand the creed I and my men live by. To us, no retribution is futile. We live only for the next fight. Isn't that why we're in the business we're in?"

"You maybe. Me, it's the money. Strictly the money. I deal with the filth I deal with because they make me a lot of money." Dominick looked down at his watch. "We have a long drive ahead of us. I think we need to leave for Owosso now."

"You're sure you want to be there when this goes down?" Starr asked.

Dominick's face hardened for an instant, then mellowed again. He stared straight into Starr's dark eyes, his voice determined and cold. "Of course I'm sure. If I wasn't, I wouldn't be going. I want to be right there in the cab of one of those eighteen-wheelers when we make the move. I want to see their faces the instant they realize we've taken their prized possession away from them. But more than that, Andy, I want to hear the government officials explain it when the media learns about the severity of the loss."

Marc lay stretched out on the motel bed, stripped to his underwear. Beside him within arm's reach lay his unsheathed Smith & Wesson 5906 9mm automatic. The TV was tuned to CNN. He watched and listened, but more than anything, he relaxed.

Carl emerged from the bathroom, and a cloud of steam swept into the room from his shower. He finished drying himself as he walked toward his double bed. "What's happening in the world, bro?"

"More of the same. The names and places change, but the stories stay the same," Marc said without taking his eyes off of the TV.

Carl rubbed his head hard with the towel and reached for a T-shirt. "Yeah, all that mess in Europe worries me."

"How so?" Marc asked.

"After all these years as the world's number-one hardcase, suddenly, without warning I might add, Ivan starts backing down. Communist satellite countries fall from the great red orbit. It all sounds just too damned convenient to me. Ivan may have changed his face, but his heart is still filled with Communist Red."

"If we plan to get any sleep tonight, that's one subject I'd better leave untouched," Marc replied. "You know my views, and you know Ivan. I guess we'll do like the rest of the world. We'll wait and see. But yeah, you're right, it is too damned convenient. Too much change much too fast."

The macro two-tone paging signal broke the decode tone squelch on the Icom U-16 that sat on the dresser beside the TV. A voice came across the speaker the instant the tone stopped. "Pathfinder, this is Barnburner. Urgent traffic. Reply on Delta uplink ComSat-D."

Marc rose from the bed and walked to the dresser. He picked up the Icom and switched to the designated channel for Delta uplink into the ComSat-D Nationwide Defense Department radio repeater system that provided a lifeline for the Highway Warriors anywhere in the Western Hemisphere through the ComSat-D orbiting communications satellite 25,000 miles in outer space. He turned and glanced over at Carl. "Must be something good if he wants us on Delta uplink. It's got the fancy ultraencryption board in it. Maybe they've found something."

"Could we be so lucky?" Carl said as he finished dressing.

Marc keyed the transmitter on the U-16. "Barnburner, this is Pathfinder on Delta uplink. You have traffic?"

The signal linked with the on-board repeater in the Leeco high-tech overroad rig parked outside the motel room. There, the Harris transceiver encoded the signal with a highly sophisticated digital encryption that changed at 2400 baud on a computerized handshake aboard the satellite. The Delta uplink was the most secure in the system. It was estimated that the most sophisticated computer system known to man would need 99.7 years to decode the encryption if it could capture and retain the transmitted signal for the duration of that time period. Then the signal was fed through a waveguide to the flat K-band antenna mounted on the roof of the armored Leeco trailer. When the Harris was in use, the repeater links throughout the country could be avoided. The signal was transmitted directly to the satellite. Marc's voice made the 25,000-mile journey to the top-secret bird and returned to earth at Delta Force command three stories below ground inside the Pentagon in Washington.

A voice crackled across the Icom speaker. "Marc, this is General Rogers. We have a new development in a serious problem. A freighter carrying a processed load of plutonium for use at the experimental lab in the Upper Peninsula has disappeared. We suspect it was hijacked by the same people who stole the PNDs. I have a fax package ready to transmit to you as soon as you can activate your radio fax. Everything you need to know should be in there. Once you get it and assess the info, call me with any questions you might have. Over."

Marc gave Carl a puzzled look, then keyed the transmitter. "General, any idea when this ship disappeared or where they would take it?"

"Negative, Marc. All we know is it's missing. The president has been notified, and to say the least, he's quite upset. He wants the plutonium back, and he wants those PNDs before they're used or traded to some unfriendly government."

"Affirmative, General," Marc said. "Is anyone else working on this?"

"Just the usual. FBI, military intelligence, that sort of thing. We have to leave them on it to keep from arousing suspicions about your existence. Don't let that bother you. You've got the ball, and authorization from the very top to proceed as you deem necessary. Whatever you need you've got. All you have to do is make the call. There's only one rule. Return the devices and the plutonium to govenment control with as little risk to civilians as possible. Over."

"We'll look over your package and get back to you on it before the night's over," Marc said.

"Great," Rogers said. "Now, there's more. We're moving twenty-four more PND warheads tonight. A crack security unit will be escorting a civilian convoy. We are working under the assumption that whoever the thieves are, they know of the existence of these devices as well. I should remind you that tactical use of these things could have irreversible consequences for our country. I speak not only of the death toll but of political ramifications around the world. These units are not supposed to exist."

"Do you want us on the security detail?" Marc asked.

"No, it's too risky. We don't want you exposed. I think the men we have on it can handle the job. Hopefully there'll be nothing to worry about."

"When does the shipment leave?"

"In a couple of hours," Rogers said. "We haven't made the time firm yet, for security reasons."

"Roger, General. The hardcases at the trucking terminal weren't extremely helpful last night. We're moving at first light to check the locations they gave us. It's not much, but it's a start. Over."

"Affirmative. I know you men will handle this situation to the liking of the Boss," Rogers said.

Marc and Carl looked at each other, but didn't speak. Their faces said it all. Marc lifted the Icom. "Affirmative. I'll set the remote receiver in the rig for your fax transmission. Give me one minute from the time we clear this frequency and then go ahead. Is that a roger?"

"That's roger," General Rogers said. "If you get in a tight spot, I can have the Delta One active and with you within an hour. You call it, it's your game. Over."

"Roger," Marc said. "We'll stay in touch. Pathfinder clear."

Marc immediately changed channels on the sixteen-channel Icom U-16. He transmitted a Dual-Tone Multifrequency signal to the remote receiver in the Leeco trailer. A beep sounded through the Icom's speaker. Marc entered a sequential tone string, and another beep sounded a second after he released the *transmit* switch. "That should take care of it," he said. "I'll get dressed and go out to the rig to retrieve it."

"I'll do it," Carl said quickly. "I'm already dressed. You hang loose and keep an ear on the radio just in case there's additional traffic."

"No argument from me," Marc said. He switched the Icom back to the paging frequency and put it on the dresser beside the television.

Carl slipped his Smith & Wesson 5906 under his shirt and left the room.

Marc settled back on the bed. He ran the possibilities

through his mind, ignoring the background noise of CNN. Several minutes passed, and Carl returned to the room carrying a computerized fax printout. "What's it say, bro?" Marc asked.

"It says we got bad troubles," Carl said as he leafed through the printout.

"How so?"

"There was enough plutonium in that shipment to build one thousand PND warheads." Carl sat on the edge of his bed and continued to thumb through the printout.

"Great," Marc replied. He sat up on the bed.

"The lab used to develop these things is located on a farm northest of Owosso. They raise sunflowers there for a cover."

"Owosso?" Marc asked. He was excited. "That's where the guy at the terminal said Dominick might be going."

"Damn," Carl said, and dropped the fax report. "He's gonna hit it."

"Let's roll." Marc scrambled for his clothes. "I'll get on the horn to the general as soon as we get on the road."

Andy Starr liked the smell of battle and the taste of blood, as long as it wasn't his. He drove a quarter mile behind the last rig in the military-civilian convoy. The convoy had left the isolated country farm outside Owosso and traveled backroads until it reached I-75 south of Saginaw. Then they had turned north on the interstate highway and immediately reached the posted speed limit. Starr left the small handheld radio on his lap and waited for the word from Tommy Dominick in the lead vehicle.

Dominick rode shotgun in the passenger seat. He occasionally leaned forward to check the rearview mirror. Pete Siberg drove the eighteen-wheeler, maintaining a narrow lead on the convoy to avoid suspicion. The cab of the rig was jet black, and the trailer bore the name ANDERSON CARTAGE COMPANY.

Dominick knew the construction zone was approaching. He carefully scanned the traffic behind him. Fortunately, it was light except for the five-vehicle convoy. A sign appeared: ROAD CONSTRUCTION—3 MILES AHEAD. "Okay, Pete, get this thing rolling. It's time."

Siberg pushed the pedal, and the rig gained speed. He held it until he reached seventy-five miles per hour. On the road ahead now he could see the flashing warning lights of the construction area. He slowed the rig and checked the rearview mirror. The convoy was coming, but they were far behind. "Say when, boss," he said as the rig approached the first barricades.

"Just north of that overpass," Dominick replied.

"Got it," Siberg said. He coasted the rig now until it cleared the overpass. Then he slammed on his brakes and skidded until the rig almost jackknifed. He looked over his left shoulder and saw no traffic between him and the convoy.

Dominick picked up his handheld radio and pressed the *talk* switch. "We're in position. When they slow, make your move."

"Affirmative," Starr said. He pressed the accelerator on the rig and moved in closer to the last unit in the convoy.

Dominick's rig effectively blocked the interstate highway. One lane was closed with heavy steel-reinforced concrete barriers separating the construction lane from the traffic lane. There was an embankment beyond the barricades and a deep median separating the north and south lanes.

"Let's do it," Dominick shouted.

Siberg rolled from the rig and moved into a position of cover behind one of the concrete barricades. Dominick was behind him. He lifted a disposable rocket rube to his shoulders and sighted on the lead truck of the convoy.

"Don't get edgy, Pete. Give 'em time. When they're on us, open fire."

Siberg drew a deep breath and held his finger nervously on the trigger. He mentally calibrated the distance and initiated a countdown. "Okay, boss. Five seconds. Four. Three. Two."

The convoy's lead rig unexpectedly screeched to a halt, and men carrying M-16s appeared suddenly from nowhere.

"We were set up!" Dominick screamed into the handheld radio.

The loud *whoosh* of the rocket leaving the tube drowned out his voice. And then the night was alive with gunfire.

Chapter Four

□ □ □

Carl drove the Leeco high-tech overroad rig while Marc rode shotgun and operated the electronic command console. Both Highway Warriors were still tired from the fight at the trucking terminal. They had longed for the comfort and rest of a night in a quiet motel, but the evildoers didn't rest. That alone kept the ex–Delta Force commandos on constant guard. Now, with the remaining top-secret PNDs moving and Tommy Dominick and his band of hardcases on the loose somewhere in Michigan, the Highway Warriors would know no rest this night. But that seemed to be more the rule than the exception since the onset of the never-ending war.

Carl shifted the overroad rig through the gears as he gained speed. The custom-built diesel engine whined, and funnels of black smoke shot from the chrome stacks that lined the side of the candy-apple-red conventional cab. Wind sheered off of the integral foil and created a slipstream over the top of the trailer as the mighty machine chewed asphalt and spat out white lines behind them.

Marc worked the channel selector on the Icom V-100 VHF transceiver and activated the priority channel that would link him to Delta Force Command in Washington. He hoped General Rogers would still be there. "Barnburner, this is Pathfinder. Do you copy on Delta uplink? We have priority traffic. Over."

There was a pause followed by the crunching sounds of the squelch tail as the repeater linked through the ComSat-D satellite. Then the Icom's speaker rattled with the sound of the control operator's voice from deep within the secure confines of the Pentagon. "Pathfinder, stand by for relay of priority traffic per SOP twenty-one. Over."

"Roger, Barnburner. Pathfinder standing by," Marc said into the microphone.

"We're a good hour away from Owosso," Carl said as he grabbed another gear and pressed hard on the accelerator.

"Maybe we can stop the move and alert the military security forces before Dominick has a chance to hit."

"God, I hope so," Carl said. Ahead of the rig now, the halogen headlights cut through the dark Michigan night, and Carl watched the area far in front as he drove.

Marc leaned to the switches on the console and activated the Collision Avoidance System (CAS) and the Obstacle Detection System (ODS) on the high-tech machine. "If a bona fide crazy like Tommy Dominick gets his hands on the additional warheads and the plutonium, we could be in for a nasty ride on this one."

"Think positive, bro. Maybe we'll be lucky and get to the research-and-development site before Dominick and his boys arrive. Could we be lucky enough to have a snare already in place when he sticks his nasty head through the loop?"

"It doesn't usually go that way, and you know it. Dominick has come this far. He knows what he's doing, and he knows why he wants the PNDs. If we don't get him at the sunflower farm, we're going to have to flush him some other way. Right now, though, I'll be damned if I know what that way is."

The Icom V-100 speaker crackled with the familiar sound of General A. J. Rogers's voice. "Pathfinder, this is Barnburner. What is your traffic? Over."

"Roger, General. We believe, determined from the information we received from our efforts last night, that Dominick and his band are going to hit the PND site tonight. We're on our way there now. Over."

"Too late for that, men. I was on another tactical frequency when you called. The PNDs are mobile now in a heavily armed convoy on their way to the Upper Peninsula. They're under some kind of aggressive action as we speak."

Marc took a deep breath, then shot a glance at Carl. He lifted the microphone. "What kind of aggressive action and where, General?"

There was a pause, and then Rogers's voice came across the speaker again. "The last part first, Colonel. The convoy is northbound on Interstate Seventy-five just south of Saginaw. They have reported shots fired about two minutes ago. What is your location?"

"We were on our way to Owosso, but we'll be changing course immediately. We're heading for Saginaw and I-Seventy-five. Can you keep us updated while we're rolling?"

"Affirmative," Rogers replied. "I'll try to give you an update every five minutes or as often as I receive them from the communications officer in the convoy. I have federal agents and local police rolling on this one, so when you get close, watch yourselves."

Carl took his eyes off of the highway for an instant and glanced over at Marc. "Got to be Dominick and his forty thieves."

"Got to be," Marc agreed. He lifted the microphone. "General, we'll pull a map on the computer screen. We're too far out to be of any use, but keep us posted, and if Dominick makes a mad run, maybe we can be there."

"My report from the scene says the highway is blocked, Colonel. Traffic is backing up tremendously fast. From what I can gather by radio, the situation is escalating into a full-blown firefight. If we lose those PNDs . . . well, you know the rest. The devices are still in an experimental stage. We aren't sure of their overall stability. If even one of those things should happen to detonate, a certain chain reaction would result. The finale could be catastrophic for the entire northeastern United States. And I won't even speculate on the reaction of the world community."

"Affirmative," Marc said. His voice was emotionless, but his gut churned from just the thought of the lethal potential riding in the convoy. He moved switches on the console and activated the computer's main menu. When he found what he wanted, he activated the video-enhancement program to retrieve a detailed topographical map of Michigan from the computer's hard-disk storage system in the Leeco trailer. In the time it took him to remove his finger from the key, the map appeared on the Super VGA color screen. Marc spoke once more into the Icom microphone. "General, can you give us coordinates of the convoy? Over."

Rogers's voice crackled through the speaker. "Affirmative. If you'll ready your equipment and stand by, I'll transmit a packet cluster with the entire course of the convoy and relevant coordinates. Over."

"Roger that, General. Give me ten seconds and transmit the data," Marc replied. He readied the hard-disk storage to receive the packet-radio data transmission. When the signal was received, the correct coordinates would be incorporated into the Michigan map. The path of the convoy would then be displayed as a red-lined overlay on the computer screen. Marc could then program the on-board computer to track the convoy's route automatically.

Seconds passed, and then the red line appeared on the screen to enhance the highways shown there. Marc entered the location of their own rig and waited until the computer calculated the time necessary to arrive at the last known location of the military convoy.

"How's it look, bro?" Carl asked.

"Twenty-three minutes, best case," Marc replied.

"Not good," Carl said as he guided the Leeco rig on the computer-directed course toward the fiasco on Interstate 75 south of Saginaw. Toward potential nuclear disaster.

"No, not very good at all," Marc agreed. "Only madmen would try to steal those PNDs and the plutonium. And from what I've seen so far, Tommy Dominick and his followers certainly qualify as that. They're all madmen, and that alone makes them very, very dangerous. We have to stop them before they turn half of Michigan into wasteland."

Action on Interstate 75 had escalated. Rather than a small skirmish, the firefight was now a full-scale battle.

Tommy Dominick still crouched behind the heavy concrete barrier, seeking cover from the fire returned by the security personnel riding with the convoy. Pete Siberg readied another projectile for the rocket tube as he lay sprawled out on the cool ground behind another concrete barrier ten feet from Dominick.

Gunfire filled the night sky as heavily armed men spilled from the rigs and lined the side of the highway. They sought any cover they could find to shield themselves from the onslaught of hostile hot-metal scorchers sent their way from Dominick's Russian-made 7.62 x 39 assault rifle.

Captain Michael Cox led the security team. He stayed low behind a concrete barrier on the opposite side of the highway from Dominick and his heavy firepower. Cox was a ten-year veteran of Army Intelligence and a dedicated career man who knew his job well. He had prepared himself for a moment just such as the one he found himself in now, but with hostile fire raining on him and his men, he suddenly realized there was a major difference between training and the reality of a firefight.

Cox shouted orders as he watched the lead cab in the eighteen-wheeler convoy smolder into a pile of twisted metal and charred flaming debris. "Edwards, take two men and move to the right flank. Hodge, you take two and go for the left. Thompson, you and four men light up the middle. Keep the grazing fire rolling toward those muzzle flashes. I don't want those men to be able to move. Keep 'em penned down until we can neutralize them. Scaletti, keep eight men around the perimeter of the trailer with the cargo. Anything or anyone moves toward it, cut 'em to ribbons. That trailer must not be compromised under any circumstances. Where's the driver of the cargo van?"

"Over here, Cap'n," Billy Arnold yelled.

"Okay, Arnold, move toward me. Keep your head down and your butt up, or those bastards are liable to shoot it off."

Arnold followed Cox's order and moved toward the concrete barrier Cox was using for cover from the hellstorm. When he reached Cox, he was out of breath, and blood oozed from scratches on both elbows from the rough pavement. "Talk to me, Cap'n," Arnold said breathlessly.

"Is there any way you can see to get that rig rolling and move either way?" Cox asked.

"Not a damned way in the world, Cap'n, unless you got some wings to get her airborne. Heavy barriers to the left. A burning wreck in front of her and a hell of a traffic mess behind. Of course, there ain't no way we can climb the barricades to the right and get up an embankment as steep as that one. Best I can tell, we got our asses pinned in, and we ain't leavin' until somebody clears that wreckage."

"Could the rig move one of these concrete barricades and make it into the median?" Cox asked.

"Hell no," Arnold said. "Not a prayer. That bastard over there, whoever he is, would stick one of them missiles right up your nose before you could get the rig a hundred feet."

Scaletti ceased firing and pressed his back firmly against the concrete barricade. He turned and faced Cox in the darkness. "He's right, Cap'n. We're hemmed in here like a closet. They ain't leavin' and we ain't leavin' until one of us runs out of ammo or trigger fingers. I say we let the flank teams move into position and make a strong counter-attack. We got the firepower and the manpower. Let's waste the assholes."

"Too risky and too early," said Cox. "We don't know how many men they have or what other surprises they have tucked away behind that barricade. I say we sit tight and see what comes. We have civilian help on the way, state police, and federal agents. We need to find a way to get them in here. Get some intel from the rear, and let's see what traffic looks like. Either these guys knew what they were doing, or they sure picked the best damned possible spot for a hit with a kiss from Lady Luck."

Scaletti dropped the magazine from his M-16/A2 and slammed a new one up the well. "I'll have my men keep the heat on while the flank teams get in place. I think we can take 'em, Cap'n. We can't sit here all—"

Scaletti's words didn't have a chance to clear his throat. A loud explosion and a massive ball of fire turned the concrete barricade into jagged chunks of lethal high-velocity shrapnel. The last thing Scaletti saw was the shredded body of Captain Cox, airborne, with a twisted look of horror contorting his face. Then the world was on fire all around him, and there was silence in the midst of the bright flash.

On the opposite side of the road, Tommy Dominick spoke into his handheld radio. "Do it now!" he yelled as the fireball across the highway dissipated into the dark Michigan sky.

Andy Starr received the message and broke his cover. He had been silent, an ace in the hole waiting for the right time to make his lethal move. And that opportunity came on the towering tail of fire from Siberg's missile. "Move out!" he yelled to the dozen heavily armed hired hardcases who surrounded him.

Starr's men moved fast. They jumped from their cover and charged the trailer housing the top-secret PNDs. Gunfire roared as tongues of fire spat from their weapons. The lethal pellets chewed into the flesh and bones of the eight men guarding the trailer.

Across the median, in the southbound lane, the revolving blue lights of a police car settled to a brutal stop. A lone man, armed with a shotgun, climbed from the driver's side of the car. He ran for the median and the northbound lane. When he reached midway, a long burst of machine-gun fire raked the ground around him.

The lawman dropped to his knees and returned fire. His efforts were far too little and much too late.

Another burst of hellfire streaked from hostile muzzles in the hands of Starr's shooters. The sizzling pellets streaked through the night and tore through him like lightning bolts dealt by the unforgiving hand of the Grim Reaper. And as his last futile load of buckshot penetrated the night sky, the great dark scythe of eternity harvested him.

The shooters moved toward the center trailer in the convoy. Toward the personal nuclear devices.

There was more gunfire now. Streaks of death lit the night from a previously quiet and darkened barricade. The right-flank team.

Starr opened fire, his full-auto AK-47 chattering. Hot

brass pelted the ground as scorching hornets sought human flesh but found none.

The clatter of a hand grenade slapped the pavement.

Starr hit the hard surface and covered his head.

An explosion roared from the exploding pineapple, and two of Starr's shooters sailed into the darkened sky. Into the arms of their Maker.

The right-flank team led by Sergeant Edwards moved toward Starr's position. Deafening gunfire roared while thick black smoke from the burning rig shrouded the area with an acrid blanket that burned everyone's lungs with each breath.

But the team charged on.

Starr was up now, his AK seeking a target and his ears ringing from the grenade explosion. Hellfire belched from the muzzle of the AK and sent 7.62mm death merchants into the darkness. Starr felt his eyes burning as the heavy smoke from the fire met sweat dripping from his brow. But that merely bolstered his determination to prove to his men and Tommy Dominick what real men were made of.

Starr fired at the muzzle flashes coming toward him out of the darkness. He heard a scream.

One down.

More gunfire now as 5.56mm tumblers sparkled through the night and slapped harmlessly into the heavy concrete in front of Starr.

Starr moved the muzzle in a sweeping arch. Deathfire swept the highway in front of him.

Another scream pierced the night over the roar of gunfire when a military security man caught a burst of 7.62 x 39 scorchers. His body spiraled to the pavement, illuminated by the light of the burning overroad rig.

Starr was moving now. He ran to his left, toward the rig carrying the PNDs, staying low behind the barricades.

Then he suddenly stopped when he spotted the silhouette of a shooter crouched behind the cover of one of the huge tires at the end of the eighteen-wheeler's trailer.

The silhouette moved and shouldered his weapon.

Andy Starr dropped to one knee and instinctively unleashed a burst of full-automatic manstoppers from the AK. Streaks of fire riveted the end of the trailer, the tire, and the shooter. The silhouette slumped forward, and a burst of wasted gunfire blasted into the pavement.

Starr was back on his feet and running now. He moved stealthily in the darkness, crouched low and avoiding as much light from the burning rig as he could. He motioned to four of his troopers to follow.

The small group gathered and waited for Starr's command. "Take the rig. I want the PNDs. Get to them and get ready to move everything into Dominick's truck. Watch your backsides. There are more security people out there in the darkness somewhere. On my handsign, move out. Everybody got that?"

All four nodded.

Starr took one final look around, saw nothing moving, and lifted his left hand.

The hardcases behind him were up and running on his order. They ran behind Starr until they reached the end of the trailer in the middle of the convoy.

Starr stopped and double-checked to be sure the silhouette at the back end of the trailer was indeed dead. He was.

"Okay, get the doors open and prepare to unload those things. I'll cover while you guys make the move," Starr said. He lifted the handheld radio from his belt and called Dominick. "We're moving the goods, Dominick. Get the end of your trailer open."

"Movin'," Dominick replied over the radio.

The gunfire had ceased. Starr scanned the area, searching for shooters. There were none visible.

"We can't get the lock off, boss," one of the hardcases said.

"Use the bolt cutters," Starr replied without looking back.

"We tried. It won't budge," the guy replied.

"Shoot the son of a bitch, then. Just get it off and get those crates out of there before the world comes swarming down on top of us. We ain't got all night." Starr caught himself growing more apprehensive with each passing second. And the fact that there was no more visible resistance worried him.

"Whatever," the hardcase said. A loud short burst of full-auto gunfire erupted, and shards of flying metal spiraled into the night. "That did it."

The hinges on the trailer's doors squeaked when the men opened them. Two of Starr's men retrieved small flashlights from their pockets and shone them into the trailer. Inside sat a dozen wooden crates with distinct markings for positive identification. Each crate was stamped TOP SECRET on the ends, sides, and top.

Starr turned and glanced into the trailer. He saw the markings on the crates, and a broad smile creased his hard face. "Bingo!" he said. "Get 'em moving. Make the transfer in three minutes or less."

The handheld radio on Starr's belt crackled.

Tommy Dominick's voice came from the speaker. "We're ready on this end," he said.

Starr grabbed the radio. "Be there in a minute. What happened to the hostiles?"

"Either dead or hiding. Maybe the survivors have had enough. I like it," Dominick said, his voice arrogant and confident.

"Right," Starr replied. He turned back to the men moving the crates. "It's clear. Make the move."

The first man jumped from the end of the trailer, and another slid the edge of the crate over the rear lip. He had started sliding the heavy wooden box when a torrent of hellfire came sailing into the trailer from the darkness.

Starr dropped to his knees and returned fire at the unseen shooters. His AK threw copper-jacketed lead into the darkness, but the hellfire didn't stop. A half-dozen rounds slammed into the hardcase inside the trailer. He slumped over, his dying scream one of painful disbelief. When he fell, so did the crate. It slammed from the trailer and hit the ground with a fierce thud, the wooden packaging splitting open. The contents fell to the pavement beside Andy Starr. Then the body of the dead man fell beside it. His flashlight flew from dead fingers and landed beside the crate. Its beam shone brightly on the contents of the crate.

Andy Starr gasped. "My God, we *have* been set up," he mumbled. "There's nothing in here but cast-iron pipe. Let's get out of here," he shouted to the men in the trailer. "Run for Dominick's rig. It's a setup."

The men jumped from the trailer and ran, but gunfire from the darkness mowed them down.

Andy Starr ran as hard as he could, the churning black smoke from the burning lead rig choking him with each step. He had Dominick's rig within sight. He glanced behind him and saw no one. Not one of his men had made it. He looked in front of him again and saw Siberg and Dominick climb aboard the cab of the rig. He was fifty feet from the cab now, but his lungs throbbed from the acrid smoke and his head pounded with fear. He ran hard, as hard as he had run in his life. Every survival instinct in his body was working double-time, and he knew he would make it. He heard the sound of the diesel cranking as he ran alongside the trailer. Then gunfire seemed to shatter the darkness from every direction, and the night was a sea of hellfire.

Chapter Five

The red direction-guidance line on the on-board computer screen continued to move as Carl steered the high-tech Leeco rig through the night over Michigan backroads.

"What's the best estimate of arrival time, bro?" Carl asked.

"Assuming the General's coordinates were correct, I would guess nine or ten minutes," Marc replied.

"Think we need to get an update from the good general?" Carl asked. He stared through the windshield into the dark Michigan night while the rig devoured pavement.

Marc lifted the Icom V-100 microphone and pressed the *talk* switch. "Barnburner, this is Pathfinder. Over."

The squelch tail sounded, then General Rogers's voice blared from the Icom speaker. "Pathfinder, Barnburner here. Go with your traffic."

Marc spoke into the microphone. "General, we're nine or ten minutes away from the destination given by your coordinates. Can you give us an update? Over."

"Nothing new, Colonel. I'll try to reach the field team and see what the status is. Over."

"Roger," Marc said. He laid the microphone on his lap

and stared out at the highway. His mind wandered to what might lie ahead. Detonation of an offensive nuclear device, even one as small as a PND, would create chaos in the United States. Perhaps even the world. The device was capable of leveling an area the size of a square city block, but the political fallout would have much greater significance.

"You're being too quiet, bro," Carl said.

"Just thinking," Marc replied.

"About what?"

"About what's around the next curve. Over the next hill. Who'll start the next global war. Will it be some deranged fanatic like Dominick who does nothing unless it's profitable? Or will it be some Mideastern hothead who manages to get his hands on the technology to exterminate millions of people with the push of a button. And will it all come down to some kook like Dominick who provides anything to anyone if the price is right?"

Carl opened his mouth to reply, but the Icom speaker made him save his thoughts. "Pathfinder, this is Barn-burner. Do you copy? Over."

"Roger, General, go ahead with your traffic," Marc said.

"Casualties are high. We've lost much of the security team, and the hostiles have incurred heavy losses also. I don't have exact numbers. It was hard to read the radio traffic because of all the gunfire. It's going down hot and heavy as we speak. Over."

"Affirmative," Marc said. "We're six minutes away. If your people can keep the hostiles engaged until we get there, we'll come in swinging with some heavy firepower. Over."

"Last report said the hostiles were making a run for their rig. It could all be over when you get there, Colonel."

Marc hesitated. "If they can find a way to contain them until we get there, we'll do the mop-up."

"Look at the sky, bro," Carl said. He stared northeast of the rig at the brilliantly glowing sky.

"Damn," Marc said. "Looks like hell's broken loose over there. That must be the place."

"Think it might be a good idea to activate the weapons systems?" Carl asked.

"Yeah," Marc replied. He moved switches and energized the electronic armaments system. The armament control panel appeared as a window on the computer screen in an overlay covering the topographical map of central Michigan. Marc verified the activation of each device and cleared the window from the screen. "We're on," he said.

Carl entered I-75 at the entrance ramp and headed north. The rig reached sixty-five miles per hour as a slowly winding curve approached. Halfway into the curve, Carl slammed on the brakes. "Shit!" he yelled.

Marc braced himself against the dashboard while Carl swerved hard into the edge of the median. The CAS beeped a shrill warning and aided Carl in avoiding a collision with two eighteen-wheelers stopped in a line of traffic in each lane of the highway.

The Leeco rig bucked and groaned as it left the regularly traveled portion of the highway and bounced through the median. The rig skidded and dropped speed, but not enough for Carl to regain control. They slid crablike toward the drainage ditch at the center of the median. Then the giant Leeco hit the ditch, listed hard to the left, and the right tires rose from the ground beneath them. For an instant, time seemed suspended while the rig hung balanced only on its left tires.

The fire of hell was all around him, but Andy Starr kept running. The rig was moving now, and Tommy Dominick leaned from the passenger's window with his automatic weapon blazing toward the source of the gunfire that sought to destroy them.

Starr reached into the darkness toward the railing on the side of the rig. He stretched his fingers and almost touched it but missed. His honed survival instincts were racing at full throttle. He ran harder than he had ever run before. His lungs ached, and every muscle in his body throbbed, but he pushed himself and stretched farther. This time, his fingers found the cool chrome metallic handrail. He grabbed it and pulled himself to the first step on the running board.

The rig shook hard as Siberg changed gears, and the jolt almost caused Starr to lose both his balance and his grip. Gunfire from the security team pelted the door beside him, but he held on tightly for his life. His outstretched right arm still held the blazing AK-47. In desperation, he sent 7.62mm death merchants into the darkness in pursuit of human flesh, but the shots went wild and found none.

Siberg grabbed another gear, and the rig jerked hard once more. Starr held tightly while the giant rig gained momentum and sped away from the hit gone bad.

Behind Siberg's rig, four of Starr's men had managed to make their way back to their own. Dick Craft managed to climb aboard on the driver's side and fire the overroad machine. He crammed the rig into gear and stomped the accelerator . The diesel groaned, the trailer shuddered, and the rig shot forward in a burst of power.

Lynn Newburg was on the passenger's side, firing at the muzzle flashes behind the concrete barricades on the right side of the highway.

Craft floored the accelerator and grabbed another gear, but there was nowhere for him to go. He hit the rear of the rig blocking the highway in front of him. The big Peterbilt listed hard right, slammed into the concrete barricades, and came to rest against the convoy rig. Craft found reverse, but the rig was wedged tightly between the trailer of the convoy machine and the concrete barricade. "Run for it!" he yelled. It took great effort, but he managed to open the driver's door and make a mad dash for safety somewhere in the median.

Lynn Newburg and the other two hardcases followed immediately, but the remnants of the security troops were closing fast now. Newburg hit the pavement on the run while gunfire peppered the pavement behind him. He spun fast, his AK-47 chattering toward the security forces. The specially trained soldiers were undaunted by the gunfire. They moved faster toward the stranded rig. Newburg took the first available cover near the end of the convoy trailer. The security troops saw him and returned fire again. Newburg unleashed a long burst from the AK and fired out the magazine. He reached for another in his belt, but the troops were moving too fast. A hailstorm of automatic weaponfire chewed through his flesh and sent a sea of blood flying into the darkness. Newburg twitched spasmodically for a long moment. Then his eyes stared into the dark Michigan sky. Sealed by death, they saw nothing.

The two men who had left the rig behind Newburg had no chance. They ran hard, their autoguns firing in total desperation into the darkness surrounding them. Their survival instincts were far too slow. A swarm of deadly hornets emerged from the darkness and stung the life from them.

Dick Craft had managed to find his way to safety despite the carnage behind him. He lay low inside the narrow drainage ditch in the center of the median and waited. He knew he had no chance of escape without adequate transportation. Traffic was nonexistent on the southbound lane. Craft surmised that someone had stopped it north of the attack point, that everyone on the highway for many miles north and south of the attack point who had a CB radio would be aware of the attack. And that meant that police, and he could only guess who else, knew of the attempted hit. That thought was of no comfort, so he let it pass. Craft looked around, searching for transportation. And then it hit him. He had overlooked the obvious, the police car. He looked at the car still sitting on the side of the highway with the blue lights still revolving. He judged the distance to the car to be about one hundred yards. He made one more search of the darkness for security troops, saw none, and started crawling.

Andy Starr swung the cab door open and climbed inside. His right hand, holding the AK-47, came in last. Tommy Dominick moved over to make room for him. Siberg concentrated on driving the rig. The CB radio was turned up loud, and there was continuous chatter, mixed frequently with obscenities and complaints about the blocked highway.

"Jeez, Siberg, turn that shit down. I'm at the brink of pissin' in my pants, and you're listening to the friggin' CB," Starr yelled.

"Hey, wise-ass, we can gather information about police and that kind of crap on this thing. Back off. You're the brains who guaranteed this thing would go down without a hitch. Why don't you just shut the hell up," Siberg said. "I got my hands full drivin' this thing, and if you don't like the noise, get the hell out."

Starr looked hard at Siberg, but he said nothing.

"Okay, you two, cut the shit," Dominick said. "We got enough troubles now as it is. What the hell went wrong back there, Andy?"

"They set our asses up, that's what went wrong. They must have known we were gonna hit. All the crates were marked correctly, but there was nothing inside but cast-iron pipe. They had our number, and all they needed was our asses. Like fools, we gave them that," Starr said. He settled in the seat and changed the thirty-round magazine in the AK.

Dominick opened his mouth to speak, but the conversation on the radio stopped him.

"Yeah, driver, I'm sayin' there's a hellground down the road. We gotta do something. Those killers are gonna cut loose and move on down the superslab in the northbound lane," the driver said on the CB.

"Damn, Pop Tart, we gotta do something to help old Smokey get 'em stopped," another driver said.

"I got me forty tons of rollin' Peterbilt," Pop Tart said. "You bring that big Five Star General over here and beside me, and we'll move some of them damned concrete bear cages into the northbound. We'll cut their asses off slicker than a cat's meow. Whatta you say about that, Mr. Stumpjumper?"

"I say let's do it and let old Smokey take care of the rest. We can stop 'em and let the devil collect his due. I like it, Pop Tart," Stumpjumper replied.

"Yeah, roger-four on that, driver. This is the old Pop Tart, and I'm amovin'. Bring yourself on up here beside me in this median. We can cross right here," Pop Tart said.

"Uh-huh, a great big ten-roger on that, Mr. Pop Tart. I'm movin' right in behind you. Get yourself crosswise the median, and I'll come along beside you," Stumpjumper said, and then the CB became so noisy with everyone trying to talk at once that no one came through clearly.

"What the hell were they sayin'?" Starr asked excitedly.

"They're saying they're gonna block the road so we can't get through," Siberg said.

"Piss on that. Turn this thing around," Dominick said.

"Okay, I'm open for suggestions," Siberg said sarcastically. "You want me to make the rig sprout wings and fly over these barricades?"

"If the highway is blocked, do we have a chance of crashing the barricades and getting through without trashing the rig?" Starr asked.

"Yeah, about as much chance as the proverbial snowball in hell," Siberg retorted.

"We can't let a bunch of redneck, do-gooder truckers stop us," Dominick said. "If we have to, we'll shoot our way out."

"Yeah, what are you gonna do then, hike back to the Dunes?" Siberg asked. "I hate to say I told you so, but when those hitters came into the terminal the other night and wiped all hell out of our people, I knew we were in deep shit. These cocksuckers have had our number since we made the first heist. It's been too damned easy."

"Don't give me that crap, Siberg," Starr said. "We've lost more than half our numbers since we started this project. That's the breaks. This ain't a cushy nine-to-five job with guaranteed retirement. Everybody came into my outfit with the same understanding: You work until you die, and you get paid very well for what you do. That includes you, Siberg. Now drive the damned truck."

Siberg was unfazed. He steered the speeding rig with skill and precision through the narrow passageway between the concrete barriers that still lined each side of Interstate 75 near Saginaw. "Starr, this mission was a mistake from the beginning. I knew it, and so did half of the men. They thought you were nuts for takin' it. I mean, look who we're dealing with on the other end. What are you gonna tell those sand-flea dickheads? You gonna tell 'em we got half the goods and they can't have the rest? You're crazy, man. They'll cut your balls off and use 'em for waterbags on the backs of their camels. Those people are whacked-out in the first place. They don't care who they're fightin' or killin' just so long as it's somebody."

"He's got a point, Andy," Dominick said. "I got to face Shirnade tomorrow. We got to stall for time, and then we have to get the rest of the PNDs. We got ten million big ones riding on this deal and no axle jockey in a big truck is gonna keep me from getting that."

"Okay," Starr said as the rig rounded a curve and the headlights shone brightly on two eighteen-wheelers in the center of the highway. In front of them sat two large concrete barricades. "Tell you what, Dominick. What say you get out of the damned truck and go tell those axle jockeys to go move their trucks."

Dominick stared through the windshield at the two rigs. Behind them in the southbound lanes, a line of traffic ran as far as he could see. "Okay, Siberg, you're at the wheel. What's it gonna be?"

Siberg let off the accelerator and slowed the rig as the barricades came closer and closer. He stopped fifty yards from the barriers and let his headlights shine on them while the rig idled. Then he reached for the CB microphone and pressed the *talk* switch. "How 'bout you over there, Stumpjumper and Pop Tart. You got a copy?"

Seconds passed, and then the strong AM signal rattled through the CB's speaker. "Yeah, roger-four, this be the Stumpjumper. Who we got there?"

"Yeah, well, Mr. Stumpjumper," Siberg said, "you got the Death Menace on this side. We be sittin' eyeball-to-eyeball with you on the other side of your little misjudgment there in the middle of the superslab. Why don't you good buddies quit playin' hero and get those things out of the roadway real quick-like before me and a few of my special friends come over on your side and kick some ass?"

Stumpjumper's laugh crackled across the speaker. Then he spoke as he caught his breath. "You ain't that tough, Death Menace. The only thing you're gonna be kickin' is the bottom end of a whole bunch of steel bars. I'll tell you something *good buddy*, Mr. Smokey is comin' for your asses."

"Too bad you won't be here to greet him, dead man," Siberg said. He let the microphone drop to the seat and kicked the cab door open with his foot. He grabbed his fully automatic Chinese AK-47 and leaned from the cab, the muzzle of the assault rifle resting across the top of the truck door. Siberg took careful aim and unsheathed a long burst of directed fire toward the rig nearest him on the other side of the barricades. When flames stopped licking from the barrel, Siberg leaned back inside the cab and picked up the microphone. "That's my diplomatic approach, dickhead. I'm gonna get real pissed in a minute, and then I'm gonna get real mean. Now get those rigs off the highway before I blow 'em off."

"I got something over here you can blow, Mr. Death Menace," Pop Tart said. "Come on out of that truck and let's see what you're made of."

"You're cute, guys," Siberg replied. "Tell you what, let it be known that I'm a generous man. I'll give you boys thirty seconds before I make scrap metal out of those rigs you're drivin'. If you're still sittin' in 'em, you're hamburger. Get your asses and those chunks of concrete out of the roadway. Play smart, and both of you heroes can go home to Mama and the kids. Think about it, and don't be a couple of dumb-asses."

There was no reply.

Starr lifted the muzzle of his AK-47 and yelled at Siberg. "Come on, let's go move those trucks." He opened the passenger door and climbed from the cab.

Tommy Dominick followed.

The Stumpjumper's voice came over the CB. "You can blow these rigs if you want to, but the highway is still gonna be blocked. You won't be goin' anywhere until Mr. Smokey gets here."

Starr made a hard face, clenched his teeth, and sprayed the front of the rig nearest him with two short fast bursts of 7.62 x 39mm scorchers. Bullets pelted into the front of the machine, and shards of glass flew onto the pavement. The second rig was a tanker. He couldn't get a clear shot at it because of the rig nearer the barricades. He gritted his teeth once more and unleashed another burst of gunfire.

Siberg lifted the microphone and spoke. "Okay, he-roes, time is almost up. What'll it be . . . death or decision?"

Handgun fire came as a reply. Three rounds smashed into the windshield of Siberg's rig, raining glass into the cab.

Siberg ducked down, grabbed his rocket tube, and jumped to the ground. He knelt by the front fender and dumped another short burst from his AK.

Starr was firing now also. Streaks of fire spat from the muzzle of his autogun as he crouched low beside the rig. Tommy Dominick knelt beside him. "Let's get it done, Andy," he said.

Starr moved backward, under the trailer. He made his way to Siberg on the driver's side of the rig, Dominick directly behind him.

Siberg turned and gestured toward them, then spoke in a whisper. "Let's take 'em. What say?"

"I say we're wastin' time," Dominick said. "We're going to have people all over this place in a few minutes. We've got to get away from here."

"You're right about that," Siberg said. He looked beyond the rigs on the other side of the barricade, and a line of at least ten sets of headlights bounced through the edge of the median. "More truckers coming. They'll block this place up so badly, we'll *never* get transportation out of here."

"Trash the lead rig," Starr said.

"What?" Siberg asked.

"I said trash the lead rig. Get the fireworks going and watch the heroics stop real quickly."

"Right," Siberg replied. He dropped the AK to the pavement and lifted the rocket tube over his right shoulder. He slid an explosive projectile into the tube and glanced back at Dominick and Starr. "You'd better get back or lay down beside me. I'm going to teach those truckers a lesson the survivors will never forget." He steadied his aim on the lead truck moving along the edge of the median.

Dominick and Starr lay prone beside Siberg. "Whenever you're ready," Starr said.

"Have a taste of hell, highway hero," Siberg mumbled, and his finger moved ever so slightly on the trigger.

Chapter Six

It had felt like forever, but the giant Leeco rig finally settled back to the ground, shuddering from the stress. Carl slammed the gearshift into groundhog low and let the clutch out slowly. The massive engine whined, and the rig moved slowly forward.

"Whew, that one was *too* close," Carl said breathlessly. He felt beads of perspiration forming on his forehead, and for the first time since he could remember, he felt himself trembling.

"You did good," Marc said. "I thought we were gone."

"Me too," Carl replied.

"Looks like we can move along the shoulder if we don't find any more hidden ditches," Marc said.

"We're going to have to stay on the shoulder until we move around some of this traffic," Carl said.

"I'll switch on the CB and see what's going on up there. We're still a couple of miles from the action according to the computer." Marc leaned to the console and flipped the switch on the CB. The speaker came alive instantly.

Carl continued to inch the rig forward along the soft grassy median of Interstate 75. He drove very carefully now as the rig gradually moved passed the long line of traffic stalled on the highway.

Then the Icom speaker rattled with General Rogers's voice. "Pathfinder, this is Barnburner. Do you copy?"

Marc lifted the Icom noise-canceling microphone from the hanger and pressed the *talk* switch. "Barnburner, this is Pathfinder. Go with your traffic. Over."

General Rogers's tired voice rattled from the speaker through the digitally encrypted ComSat-D satellite link. "Roger, Colonel. We have an update from the troops in the convoy. There are many casualties. Still no count, but people died on both sides. Some of the hitters, and we think that includes Tommy Dominick, have escaped in an eighteen-wheeler. They are moving northbound on I-Seventy-five. Our people there can't get past the wreckage of one of the convoy rigs. They have no way to pursue. Where are you now? Over."

"We're moving along the edge of the median, General. Should be about a mile or two from the site of the hit. We almost lost the rig due to traffic tie-ups. This place is a mess out here. How is traffic on the southbound side? Can you get us a report from the people at the site? Over?"

"Stand by, Marc. I'll see if the console operator still has contact," Rogers said.

"Pathfinder standing by." Marc lowered the microphone and glanced over at Carl. "You know, bro, if they get away from here, we got big-time troubles. Someone crazy enough to steal top-secret nuclear warheads just might be crazy enough to use 'em. That makes me very, very nervous."

Carl looked ahead as he continued to inch the Leeco machine forward. "Yeah, and that concrete drainage line up ahead makes me nervous."

Marc looked ahead and saw the line extending from the shoulder into the center of the median toward the drainage ditch that ran parallel to the highway. "We can clear that one if we take it nice and slow. What do you think?"

Carl didn't have a chance to answer because General Rogers's voice roared from the Icom speaker. "Pathfinder, we have more information. Traffic coming from the north seems to be at a standstill. Word is, according to the CB traffic received at the site, some truckers have blocked the road a mile or so north of the attack point. Does that help you?"

Marc pressed *talk*. "Roger, General, that means a lot. Thanks. We'll be in touch. Pathfinder clear."

Marc looked out at the concrete drainage line, then over at Carl. "You feel adventurous?"

"You mean try to take the rig across the median and that ditch down there?"

"You got it," Marc replied.

"Okay, worse come to worst, we can always offload one of the Jeeps and make a move that way. That's if we don't roll this thing."

"You're driving, Major. Do your thing."

Carl moved the steering wheel slightly to the left and let the rig roll toward the center of the median and the narrow drainage ditch. He moved slowly and deliberately, feeling each foot of earth beneath the tires as the rig moved forward. "Here we go," he said as the left front tire of the Leeco machine slipped slowly over the edge into the drainage channel.

The Highway Warriors held their breath while the Leeco rig groaned from the unusual strain and odd angles presented to the framework when the rig crawled over the hole and started to climb out the other side.

"Take it slow, bro, and I think we'll make it," Marc said. He held tightly to the door strap when the rear tires of the custom tractor pulled to climb out the other side of the ditch.

The rig creaked and groaned louder as the machine cleared the opposite side. The trailer moved over the ditch; then the rear tires slipped into it, and all forward momentum stopped. The giant diesel bogged down and groaned. Carl slammed the clutch to the floor and hit the brakes so the machine wouldn't roll backward. A disgusted look filled his face when he looked at Marc. "This is going to be interesting, bro," he said.

"You can do it," Marc said. "Just take it slow."

Carl dropped his foot from the brake and let it rest on the accelerator. He let the clutch out slowly, then pressed down on the throttle. The rig moved slightly, and the wheels started spinning. Then the tires gripped the earth and found traction. The trailer shifted, leaned, then rolled up on the other side of the ditch.

"Hot damn!" Carl yelled. "We made it." He slapped the steering wheel as the rig climbed onto the pavement on the southbound side. "I sure hope the general's info was right and traffic is stopped," he said as he grabbed another gear and headed north in the southbound lane.

"Just be cool and watch as far ahead as you can. You should have plenty of time to react if something is coming the other way," Marc said as he looked across the median at the line of vehicles stopped on the northbound side. He stared at them for a long moment and then reset the CAS and the ODS.

So far, there had been no traffic, just as General Rogers had indicated. Carl kept their speed at forty-five while he scoured the highway in front just in case the information had been in error.

Suddenly the gibberish emitted by the CB speaker was replaced with the loud roaring signal of an excited voice. "Pop Tart, run for it. The son of a bitch has a rocket launcher."

There was no reply, and the gibberish of mixed amplitude-modulated signals filled the CB speaker.

"Step on it!" Marc yelled. "It's got to be the hitters."

"I'm steppin'," Carl replied. "But if that guy saw what he thought he saw, all we're gonna be able to do is sort through the pieces."

Pete Siberg touched off the rocket round. The death missile streaked through the night toward the first rig rolling slowly down the shoulder of the highway. By the time a human eye could register the projectile, it struck the nose of the tractor and exploded. A massive hailstorm of fire and debris rained on both lanes of the interstate. A cyclonic fireball bellowed skyward in a twisting spiral. The unknown driver of the rig died instantly as the dead mammoth settled back to earth and rolled over on its side in a final death throe.

People stalled in traffic left their cars and trucks now, screaming toward the safety of the southbound side of the highway.

Pop Tart and Stumpjumper watched the melee through horror-filled eyes. At almost the same instant, they jumped from their rigs and ran north toward safety.

But there was no safety now. Andy Starr and Tommy Dominick were already running toward the rigs and the barricades. Their autoguns counted out final payment for the interference.

Stumpjumper stopped abruptly. He crouched behind the wheel of his rig and fired frantically with a 9mm automatic pistol. He couldn't see Starr or Dominick, but he spotted the silhouette of Pete Siberg illuminated by the headlights on the rig running toward the barricades. He fired three rounds, and the silhouette went down. When he saw that, Stumpjumper was up on his feet and running as hard as he could toward the median.

He almost made it into the darkness, but a long burst of automatic gunfire swept him off his feet and sent him catapulting toward the grassy divider. He couldn't feel his legs, and his lungs were on fire. He struggled for breath and tried to kick himself off the pavement into the grass. Just when he thought he had found the burst of energy necessary to do that, something inside him told him to look back. He found himself staring down the barrel of Andy Starr's AK-47.

Starr's face was chiseled in ice, but in it there was the reflection of fire from the burning rig across the median. The fire seemed to spit from his eyes. His look was expressionless when he stared down at Stumpjumper. "Which one are you, Stumpjumper or Pop Tart?"

Stumpjumper hesitated, struggled to get another breath, and looked into the fiery eyes that bored through him. "Stumpjumper," he said, although the words came with difficulty.

"You just had to be a hero, didn't you?" Starr asked.

Stumpjumper looked back at Starr with bewilderment and fear. "Who are you?" he asked.

Starr forced a meaningless smile. "I'm hell's gate-keeper. You've committed a very serious error. The cost of your mistake is quite high."

"What?" Stumpjumper asked. Although the temperature was cool, he felt himself sweating. And he still couldn't feel his legs.

"You should have minded your own business and kept driving that truck. From truck driver to worm food in one twitch of the finger. Bye, bye, hero," Starr said coldly.

Stumpjumper's eyes widened, and he trembled. And then he saw the streak of fire spit from the bore of the gun in Starr's hands. In the next instant, he saw nothing because his eyes flew from his head when the bullet struck between them.

Starr turned and ran back toward the rigs. He found Dominick near the eastern edge of the northbound lane, searching for Pop Tart. "You find him?" he asked.

"He's somewhere in the weeds on this side of the road. I can't find him in the dark," Dominick said.

"Where's Pete?" Starr asked.

"He's hit on the other side of the barricades," Dominick replied.

"Is he dead?"

"I don't think so. I heard him yell just a second or two ago. I didn't go back over there because I didn't know if the other driver was armed," Dominick said.

"Piss on the trucker. Let's check Pete." Starr ran hard toward the barricades, hurdled them, and stopped beside Siberg. Even at first glance, Starr could tell the wounds were fatal.

"Hey, Andy," Siberg said. "I took a couple of hits. I think it's bad. I got to get to a doctor or a medic or something."

Starr looked at the wounds, but his face, illuminated by the headlights of the rig, remained expressionless. One hit had caught Siberg in the upper thigh. He was bleeding profusely from the femoral artery, and his pants were soaked. A puddle of blood accumulated beneath his leg and trailed onto the pavement in a narrow streak. The second slug had caught him in the chest. The open wound there was foaming, and each time Siberg drew a pain-filled breath, the opening sucked air. A lung shot. "This is a tough break, Pete. Real tough."

"You got to help me, Andy. I'm dyin'. I can feel it. Don't let the feds get me. Wow, I'm so hot. Get me something to drink. I need a cool drink, Andy. Will you get me a medic or somebody? You got to help me, Andy."

"Yeah," said Starr. "I got to help you, Pete. I can't leave you here like this to talk. If you made it, they'd get too much out of you." He stood and let the muzzle of his AK-47 rest against the side of Siberg's head. "It's a real tough break for you, kid, but that's the way they fall sometimes." Starr squeezed the trigger before Siberg could realize what was happening. The AK roared, and Siberg's head jerked sideways while blood splattered through the night. Pete Siberg didn't move anymore. The pain was gone, and he was silenced forever.

"Jesus," Dominick said in total disbelief. "You just murdered one of your own men. I don't believe you, Starr. You must have ice water in your veins. Don't you have any compassion for anyone?"

Starr turned back toward the rigs vacated by Stumpjumper and Pop Tart. Flames from the wreckage reflected from the sides of both rigs. Black smoke now twirled in twisted tails on the wind. "Nope," he said. "Compassion will get you killed, Dominick. In this line of work, there's no room for it. You would do well to learn that, but then I figured a guy in your business would already know it. Maybe I was wrong. Besides, a wounded man is nothing more than excess baggage. We don't need that right now."

"You're an animal, aren't you," Dominick said nervously. He suddenly felt very weak and very afraid. He knew if Starr could kill one of his own as quickly as he had just killed Pete Siberg, he wouldn't hesitate to put a bullet through anyone's back if he stood to gain something by it.

"Isn't that why you hired me and my men? Or were you really looking for some Boy Scouts?"

Dominick said nothing. He turned away from the mass of torn flesh and pooling blood that seconds before had been Pete Siberg's head.

"Yeah, that's what I thought. Now let's get the hell out of here," Starr said, and he ran toward the rigs on the other side of the barricades.

"Which one?" Dominick asked. At that moment he didn't really want to go, but the guaranteed alternative if he stayed was even less attractive than Starr's brutality.

"The one without the bullet holes. The tanker. I worry about you, Dominick," Starr said as he climbed the barricades. He stopped beside the heavy stainless-steel tanker and looked once more at Dominick. "I'll drive," he said, and climbed into the driver's side of the cab.

Dominick reluctantly climbed aboard on the passenger side and settled into the seat.

Starr fired the engine and pressed the accelerator slightly after dropping the gearshift into reverse. He backed the rig straight back until he could make a sharp right turn and move into the median. Then he kicked the gearshift into low and moved slowly forward. The rig rolled across the grassy strip and came out on the southbound lane ahead of the stopped traffic and frightened late-night commuters. Starr hit another gear, and the rig headed south. A broad smile split his face. He glanced at Dominick, who sat nervously in the passenger seat. "They can't stop us now, huh, Tommy? We're rollin' hell on eighteen wheels."

Dominick was hesitant, but he finally answered, "Right, hell on eighteen wheels." And he felt butterflies churning inside his stomach because he knew Shirnade would not be so understanding.

Carl let up the accelerator when he saw the flashing blue lights atop a stopped car on the shoulder of the road. He let the rig drift with momentum as the Highway Warriors approached the patrol car.

"Infrared scanner is on," Marc said while he watched the electronic imager that surveyed the designated target area with an invisible beam of infrared light sensitive to body heat. "I don't see anybody around the car."

"Maybe he's across on the other side," Carl said. He grabbed another gear and brought the rig back up to speed as the high-tech machine rolled past the patrol car.

"Just as well," Marc said. He scoured the area around the patrol car with his naked eyes as they rolled past it. He saw nothing in the darkness except what remained of the burning eighteen-wheeler from the convoy on the northbound side of the highway. "Looks like a hell of a mess over there."

"Yeah, but where's Tommy Dominick?" Carl asked. He shifted into another gear, and the mighty custom diesel engine purred.

A slowly winding curve appeared in front of the Leeco rig. Carl let up the accelerator again for the sake of caution. The rig's high-intensity quartz halogen headlights lit the night in front of the conventional tractor with the brilliance of daylight.

"I don't understand why the enforcement agencies of the United States government let a known fanatic like Dominick continue on his course of madness," Marc said. "They've known what he's been up to for a long, long time. But the powers that be turned their heads and permitted an atrocity like this to happen. They could have taken him down long ago, but they didn't. Now look at that mess. Innocent people are dead. All because of a system that permits people like Dominick to have their freedom until they commit some extreme act of violence. Hell of it is, if the word leaks out about all this—and I'm sure it will—the news media won't focus on Tommy Dominick. Instead they'll raise hell because the United States has developed a low-yield personal nuclear device for battlefield use. What's wrong with this picture?"

"That's why we're working," Carl quipped.

The CAS alert beeped, and the ODS emitted a shrill intermittent alarm. Carl's eyes opened wide, and he acted out of reflex. He cut the steering wheel hard to the right toward the median with the electronic and hydraulic assistance of the CAS. "Here it comes," he yelled.

Ahead of the Leeco machine, headlights bore down on the Highway Warriors at high speed. From the marker lights atop the cab, Carl could see it was an eighteen-wheeler. And the driver was making no effort to slow his rig. Worst of all, the Highway Warriors had no way to know that the driver of the charging rig was Andy Starr and the passenger was Tommy Dominick.

The two rigs were heading straight for each other, but Starr still made no effort to slow the speeding tanker.

He merely growled, "Who is that crazy son of a bitch coming north in the southbound lane?"

Tommy Dominick held his breath as the rigs drew closer. "You're gonna kill us. Back it down. Please, back it down!" he screamed.

Starr ignored Dominick's pleas and stomped the accelerator. He aimed the nose of the conventional tractor for the dead center of the oncoming rig. "Let's see what this crazy son of a bitch is made of." He chuckled.

"You're gonna kill us," Dominick screamed again. "He's off on the shoulder. For God's sake, let it go."

"Shut up, Dominick. I'm drivin' this thing," Starr snapped.

Only two hundred yards separated the two rigs now. Carl watched in total disbelief as the rig seemed to aim for him. "Hang on, bro. This might be the big one," he yelled.

"What's wrong with that guy?" Marc asked.

"Pissed from sittin' in traffic, I guess," Carl said. "I got a plan. Hold your backside." He grabbed another gear on the Leeco machine and cut hard left back onto the pavement. He hit the throttle of the mighty diesel with all the thrust he could get into his right foot. The Leeco rig shot forward and gained momentum at an astounding speed.

Only one hundred yards of pavement remained between them now. Headlights blared into headlights as the two forty-ton rigs bore down on each other like Old West gunfighters in a midday showdown.

Carl gripped the wheel tightly and kept the throttle all the way down on the floorboard. He fixed his eyes on the marker lights atop the conventional tractor to avoid being blinded by the high-beam headlights that shone so brightly into his eyes.

Starr held his ground as the glare of Carl's headlights blinded him. He gritted his teeth, mumbled something unintelligible, and decided to ride the rig to death if necessary.

Fifty yards now.

Tommy Dominick screamed again. "Starr, have you gone mad? We'll all die. Let the guy pass."

"Not in this lifetime," Starr bellowed. "I'll teach him a lesson. You don't play chicken with Andy Starr. Nobody does."

Carl grabbed the air horn cord and yanked hard on it. The twin horns blared a harsh warning, but the other rig stayed on a course of sure death.

Twenty-five yards, and the threshold of evasive survival approached faster than a heartbeat.

Marc reached for the weapons control, but there was no time. Destiny had come, and death had already set its sights on the Highway Warriors. The Grim Reaper was racing toward them, cloaked in the shroud of forty tons of rolling death. "Too late," Marc yelled. "He's gonna hit us!"

Chapter Seven

□ □ □

Dave Craft stopped crawling in the center of the median drainage ditch long enough to check the area around him for any sign of security troops. He could hear voices behind him and to his right near the rig where he had narrowly escaped death. He had managed to keep low while he crawled, and that, coupled with the darkness, had probably been what had saved his life. The troops, although drastically diminished in number by the initial onslaught of the attack, still searched feverishly for any remaining hostiles. The gunfire had long since ceased, but the potential still hovered like an ominous cloud over the area.

Craft wondered who the crazy driver was in the rig that had passed by a minute or so earlier traveling north in the southbound lane. He realized he couldn't let the same impatience overtake him that had apparently overwhelmed that driver. Right now, impatience could very well cost him his life.

When he was satisfied that no troops were near, Craft lowered his head and continued to crawl toward the police car that still sat on the edge of the median, its blue lights revolving like an urgent beacon in the night. He had moved less than ten feet when he heard voices that hadn't been there a moment before. And now, they sounded very, very close. He stopped and listened. The voices *were* close. Without looking up to be sure, Craft calculated the conversation to be somewhere near the edge of the pavement, forty feet away.

Craft held his breath. His heart was beating so rapidly that it was difficult to hear what the men were saying. He tried to calm himself, tried not to do anything that would reveal his location. There was no question he was vastly outnumbered, and the last thing he needed was to engage in another firefight with the men of the convoy. To do so would mean his immediate death. And dying wasn't on his list of things to do today.

Craft remained perfectly still and waited to determine what the men would do. The conversation had not diminished, nor, from the sound of the voices, had the men moved. Time was of the essence, and if he had any prayer of escape, Craft knew he had to get to the patrol car before more authorities arrived on the scene. And without doubt, they would.

The night was mysteriously quiet now. It seemed strange to be lying in the median between the lanes of one of the busiest interstate highways in the country and not hear the constant sounds of cars and trucks. Then the voices shifted with the slight breeze that blew over the ground. Now Craft could hear them clearly.

"I swear it, Sarge. I saw one of those guys run into the median. I didn't see him cross the highway," a trooper said. "I think he's still down there somewhere."

Then the other man, the sergeant, replied, "Johnson, I think you were seeing things. It went down real fast back there. I think we got 'em all except the ones that got away in the truck."

"I still think it's worth a look," Johnson said. "I'd feel better if we took a walk through the grass down there."

Sarge shifted the position of his M-16 and motioned

toward the median. "Okay, but I think we're wastin' time. We need to mop this up before the choppers get here for the wounded. Let's make it quick."

Craft heard loose gravel shift under the men's feet as they moved toward the grass. He took a chance and moved his head to see how far away the patrol car was. Although the darkness made accurate judgment of distance difficult, he guessed it to be fifty yards, give or take ten.

He listened. The men weren't talking anymore, but he could still hear their footsteps in the grassy median. They were uncomfortably close.

Then the voices came back, this time *very* close.

"Johnson, go to the left," Sarge said. "I'll go right. Make a sweep along the ditch for fifty or so yards and come back this way. We'll meet in the middle. I still think it's a waste of time."

"Got it," Johnson replied.

Craft took a death-defying chance. He rose from the ditch in one smooth motion and stopped on his knees. He aimed his weapon instinctively. The fully automatic AK-47 in his hands spouted 7.62 x 39mm death into the darkness. He swept the kill zone in front of him with a pair of lethal figure eights. And when the death chatter stopped, he heard one man gasping.

"Sarge," Johnson yelled. Then gunfire lit the night from the muzzle of his M-16.

Craft released another burst of deathfire and fired out the remainder of the AK's magazine. He hit the mag release and let the empty fall to the ground. Instinctively, he grabbed another full magazine from his belt and crammed it into the well of the autogun. He let the bolt close and fired another burst before Johnson could find the kill zone.

Johnson spiraled toward the grass, his body twitching in its final death throes.

Craft couldn't hesitate. He was up and running without

looking back. He knew more shooters would come, and they would come fast. He moved along the dark ditch with the skill of a mountain goat. He was motivated by a fear greater than any he had ever known.

Thirty yards to go. He could here the sounds of men behind him. Then the night came alive with gunfire. But the shots weren't directed. They were randomly fired into the darkness.

Twenty yards to go. He ran past the body of the slain state trooper. The bullets hit closer now. Dirt and grassy debris sailed into the night near him. Bullets streaked past him in the darkness, so close he could hear them whistling an invitation to eternal peace. But he didn't accept. No way. He ran harder toward survival.

Ten yards. The darkness was filled with gunfire now as more and more of the surviving shooters from the convoy joined the assault. But they couldn't see him, and he had to keep it that way. Darkness was both his friend and his enemy. Craft felt his lungs burning from his efforts, and the adrenaline pumped through his system with the force of an open fire hydrant.

Five yards. Craft could almost feel the door handle in his hands. He imagined the safety of the partrol car as more and more bullets dug into the earth around him.

Three. Two. His hand touched the handle. He held the AK with his other hand and opened the door. Without thinking, he tossed the AK into the front seat, slipped behind the wheel, and dropped the gearshift into drive. He floored the accelerator, and the tires spun freely in the dew-dampened grass. Suddenly they caught and gripped the edge of the pavement. Streaks of black rubber scored the highway when the powerful Chrysler engine sent horsepower and torque to the drive shaft. The car fishtailed, swerved, then straightened in the center of the southbound lane at high speed.

Craft breathed a sigh of relief. He had made it. He had damned the odds and escaped, survived. Then a torrent of bullets cut through the body of the speeding patrol car.

Marc and Carl braced themselves for the lethal impact, but it didn't come. At the last possible second, the CAS jerked the Leeco rig out of the path of the speeding rig driven by Andy Starr. The Leeco machine slid through the median, and for an instant Carl was sure it would overturn. It didn't.

Carl cut the wheel hard to the left to straighten out. He guided the rig carefully though the median until he completely regained control, then slipped back onto the pavement and resumed his speed.

Marc was still trying to speak. After his nerves calmed, he looked at Carl, relieved. "Sorta close there, wasn't it, bro?"

"Slightly." Carl shook his head in disbelief and stared at the highway in front of them. He could see flames towering into the night, lighting the sky. There were headlights stopped in the middle of the highway as far as he could see. "This must be the place," he said.

"Weapons are ready, just in case," Marc said. He rechecked the armament display on the on-board computer. When the systems were completely functional, he reached behind his seat and retrieved his silenced Uzi. He worked the bolt and let a round feed into the chamber. Then he verified the fire selector to assure it was in a safe position. "When you stop, you sit tight. I'll get out and make the preliminary check. Keep me covered from inside. If Dominick and his rent-a-slime are still here, we could have some more fireworks real fast."

Carl let the Leeco rig coast to a stop at the road's edge. He visually checked the area. People were moving sporadically without purpose. Fire raged in the median where an eighteen-wheeler was engulfed in a torrent of black smoke. "No question about it. Dominick has been here," he said.

"I'd sure like to think he's still here," Marc said. "Sit tight, and I'll see what's going on."

"Watch your backside," Carl said.

Marc gave Carl the thumbs-up sign and climbed from the custom diesel tractor. He held the Uzi muzzle-down beside his right leg, out of sight. He moved through the firelit darkness toward a gathering of a dozen or more men standing near the median on the northbound side of the highway. He looked carefully as he approached, but the men were talking calmly, and there appeared to be no danger. That could mean but one thing. Dominick and company were already gone.

Carl watched every move Marc made. He directed the infrared imager on Marc's back and alternated his glances between the computer screen and the windshield. But from what he could see, there were no aggressors.

Marc was ten feet from the gathered men, and he could see more clearly now. There was a man down on the edge of the pavement. The other men were simply standing around him. The atmosphere was somber, the voices low and reserved.

Marc cautiously kept the Uzi out of sight. "What happened here?" he asked when he reached the gathering.

All of the faces seemed to turn and look at him in unison. No one answered at first, but then one man spoke. "Crazy bastards came up to the barricades over there. Me and Stumpjumper here tried to stop 'em. They shot the hell out of everything, and then they just murdered him. Shot him down in cold blood. One of 'em stood over him and shot him in the face after he was wounded. I got away and hid over on the shoulder. Thought they were going to kill me too. And they would have if I hadn't gotten out of sight. Who are you?"

"Call me a friendly assistant of justice. What's your name?" Marc asked.

"Pop Tart. That's my handle. Name's Jim Cannon. That's my rig over on the north side of the barricade. They shot it all to hell. What's your name?"

"Pathfinder. What happened to the people who did this?"

"They stole the Stumpjumper's rig and hauled ass south above five minutes ago."

"Damn!" Marc said. "What kind of rig, a tanker?"

"You got it, dude. Killed the man and stole his rig. Hell of a note for the safe and secure highways of America, huh?"

"Okay, you guys sit tight. Help is on the way. What happened to the burning rig?" Marc asked.

"Bastards had a rocket launcher or something. They blew it to a million pieces with one shot. Old Stumpjumper here, he got his pistol and killed the one with the rockets. He's over on the other side of the barricades, near where those dudes left their rig. Who the hell *are* these people?" Pop Tart asked.

"They're a bunch of kill-crazy fanatics. Did you see how many there were when the tanker left?"

"Two. A big guy and one a little smaller. It's the smaller one you'd better be careful around. He's the one that shot Stumpjumper in the face. He's nuts," Pop Tart said.

"Okay, guys, thanks," Marc said. "And I'm sorry about your friend."

Pop Tart looked at Stumpjumper's body on the pavement, then stared back at Marc. "All we were trying to do was help catch those crazy bastards. Where are the Smokeys when you need 'em? Damn," Pop Tart said.

"I understand," Marc said. "Smokey's doing the best he can, but he can't be everywhere at once. You guy's hang loose until help gets here. And by the way, thanks for the information." He turned and left. He walked to the barricades, climbed over them, and stopped beside the body of the man Pop Tart said Stumpjumper had shot. Marc knelt beside the body and examined the wounds in the light from the nearby rig's headlights. The man was dead, all right, but he had been shot by more than a pistol. Marc searched the body for any form of identification, found none, and ran back to the Leeco machine.

"What's the scoop?" Carl asked.

Marc laid the Uzi on the floorboard and settled in the seat. He closed the cab door and snapped his seat belt in place. "Turn this rig around and roll it hard southbound. That was Dominick in the tanker that almost took us out back down the highway. They killed the driver and stole the rig. We've got to find him before he gets off the interstate. There are two of them in the rig, and they're going to keep killing until we stop them."

Andy Starr drove hard. He kept the rig in the middle of the highway, over the centerline. He was still laughing at the chicken driver he had run completely off the highway.

Tommy Dominick wasn't quite so amused. He yelled, "You're an idiot, Starr. You would have killed us, wouldn't you. If that guy hadn't gotten completely off the road, you would've hit him. I think you've lost your mind."

Starr abruptly stopped laughing. He took his eyes off the road and looked over at Tommy Dominick. His eyes filled with fiery hate, and his voice was ice-cold. "Shut up, Dominick. I've had enough of your bullshit. From now on, I run this deal. I'll negotiate with Shirnade. I'll cut the deal. If you want to live long enough to enjoy any of the profits, then keep your mouth shut. Do I make myself clear?"

Dominick's lips tightened, and his face flushed. "You stupid bastard, you don't talk to me like that. I'm still in control of this deal." He swung the muzzle of his AK-47 up and toward Starr. He flipped the selector to full auto. "You keep smartin' off and screwin' around with me, Starr, and I'll blow you away. Your ass will be fish bait on the bottom of Lake Michigan."

Andy Starr looked straight ahead and laughed hysterically. He kept his eyes fixed on the roadway and pressed the accelerator to the floor. The rig gained speed, and for kicks, he swerved from one side of the barren highway to the other. "Shoot me, Dominick. Squeeze that trigger if you got the balls. Of course, if you do, you're in for the ride of your life. Maybe you're good enough or fast enough to get this thing stopped before it crashes into something real solid. But then again, maybe you're not. I don't think you got the balls."

Dominick froze, the muzzle aimed unsteadily at Andy Starr. He knew he was engaged in a classic Mexican standoff. His gut churned from tension and anger. After all, he was Tommy Dominick, and nobody dared talk to him that way. But now it was a lose-lose situation. And while he contemplated his options, the tanker rig rolled south on I-75 at breakneck speed.

Starr still laughed. The rig swerved back and forth across the highway like a snake. "What's it gonna be, Dominick? If you got balls, pull the trigger. If you don't, keep your mouth shut and do what I tell you."

"Stop the rig," Dominick said nervously.

"You stop it. You're the one with the gun," Starr said in a mix of words and laughter.

"I mean it, Starr. Stop the damned rig."

"You know the difference between you and me, Dominick?" Starr asked.

"Yeah. I got brains, and you're all brawn," Dominick replied.

"The difference between you and me, Dominick, is you're afraid to die and I'm not. I accepted death years ago.

And you . . . you never learned how to live, so you're afraid of dying. Think about that," Starr said.

"Maybe I am afraid of dying. No big deal. But be assured of one thing—I'm not afraid to kill. Now stop the rig," Dominick said coldly.

For the first time since the confrontation had begun, Starr shot a glance toward Dominick. He realized Dominick was deadly serious, but he decided to chance it and call his bluff. He grinned again and turned back around to look at the highway. That's when he saw the police car in front of him with flashing blue lights. The car was traveling at high speed, and like the eighteen-wheel tanker, it was all over the highway.

Starr let up the accelerator and steadied the rig, but his reaction was too slow. He was already within fifty feet of the police car, and that left him no alternative. He kicked the accelerator, and the rig gained speed again.

"What are you doing?" Dominick screamed.

"I'm taking him out. Would you rather I stop him and ask him to join us for a cup of coffee?" Starr retorted sharply.

Dominick kept the AK across his lap with the muzzle leveled at Starr's side. He chanced an occasional glance at the highway, and each time he did, the revolving lights on the police car blinded him. "How are you going to do it?" he asked.

"Crash his ass," Starr said. "You'd better hold on tight. It's going to get bumpy. Don't get too close to that trigger unless you intend to pull it, and I think we've already established the answer to that, haven't we?"

Dominick didn't say anything, but he knew Starr was right. And with the heat, the tentacle of authority, only a few feet in front of them, it was certainly no time to continue the argument. One officer alone didn't present much of an obstacle, but one officer with radio communications presented an entirely different problem. And the paramount issue of the moment was to dispose of the problem expediently and permanently.

The front bumper of the rig slammed into the rear end of the police car. The jolt from the impact shook the rig with a violent tremor. For an instant, the patrol car shot forward, but Starr kept up the assault. He moved the tanker to the right and tried to pull alongside the patrol car. It didn't work.

Dave Craft's heart raced as he steered the police car with every ounce of skill he had. The impact from the speeding eighteen-wheeler stunned him. At first, he thought it was an irate trucker. But then common sense overcame him, and he guessed it had to be some security troops who decided to give chase when he escaped from the melee in the middle of the interstate. He knew his choices had suddenly become quite limited. He could outrun the speeding rig or outdrive its driver. He also knew a two-ton car, especially one with mechanical damage from bullets, was no match for forty tons of speeding machinery. Just as that thought flashed through his mind, Craft instituted a zigzag pattern back and forth across the southbound lanes of the highway. He pressed the gas pedal all the way to the floor, and the engine sputtered. And then he looked ahead for a way out, off the highway.

Starr was unrelenting. To back off now would allow the policeman a mode of escape. And that meant trouble. He moved in close again and followed the patrol car's pattern back and forth from one edge of the pavement to the other, waiting for the right time to strike. He tried once more to move alongside the car, but the driver was cautiously defensive. He yelled at Dominick, "When the cop goes right, I'll go left and close as tightly as I can. Get your window down and shoot the tires out."

Dominick looked at Starr with a gaze of bewilderment

and contempt, but he lowered his window and shifted the muzzle of the AK until he was in a firing position. Then he waited while the rig ran a crisscross pattern on the highway.

Star closed in tight on the patrol car. He tapped the bumper again, and the driver steered hard right. Starr went left.

Gunfire roared through the cab of the tanker, and hot brass pelted the seat where Dominick sat. Screaming lead streaked from the muzzle of the autogun and slapped violently into the patrol car. A half-dozen rounds found their mark and cut through rubber on the left rear tire of the speeding car.

Dave Craft tried to control the car but couldn't. He let up the accelerator, and the speeding car careened to the left side of the highway. He jerked the steering wheel, and the car shot wildly across the highway to the right side. He looked left just as the right side of the huge tanker's cab slammed into him. The last thing he saw was Tommy Dominick's stunned face in the passenger's window of the eighteen-wheeler's cab. The stolen patrol car was now totally out of control. It left the highway at more than eighty miles per hour and plowed into the giant concrete pillar of a bridge abutment just as the speeding eighteen-wheeler shot past.

Chapter Eight

"Barnburner, this is Pathfinder. Do you copy?" Marc held the microphone and waited for the reply from Delta Force HQ inside the Pentagon.

The reply came almost immediately. General Rogers's voice sounded weary. "Pathfinder, this is Barnburner. Do you have traffic?"

Marc stared through the windshield as white lines sped by in a solid streak. "Roger, Barnburner. We are in pursuit of Dominick and at least one of his crew. They smoked an eighteen-wheeler north of the original attack site and stole an eighteen-wheel tanker. You'll find a couple more bodies up there also. These people are leaving a trail of blood in their wake. If it keeps up, they're not going to be too hard to follow. Do you have updated information? Over."

"Affirmative, Pathfinder. It's more of the same, I'm afraid. Casualties are high at the attack site. The death toll rises with each new report. Last report said three more of Dominick's hitters were terminated. One escaped after he killed two of our men. He got away in a state trooper's car. His last known direction of flight was south on Interstate Seventy-five."

Marc looked at Carl, his face filled with frustration.

"The trooper's car on the side of the highway. It had to be. There were no others around. It hasn't been long enough for something like that to happen since we came through. Damn it all."

"That makes life just wonderful. Now we have two of them to find," Carl said. He glanced down at the digital speedometer: 150 miles per hour. "Maybe we can catch them if traffic doesn't get in our way at the next exit."

Marc lifted the microphone and pressed *talk*. "Barnburner, we saw the trooper's car when we were northbound a few minutes ago. I scanned it on the infrared, and there was no one around it. He couldn't be too far ahead of us. The tanker Dominick escaped in tried to run us off the road just north of the partol car. We're rolling hard, General. We're going to try to catch them. Over."

"Okay, Colonel," Rogers said. "I still have units rolling in that direction. They should be arriving soon. I've been in contact with Agents Harrison and Crain at the bureau. They have a special interest in this also."

"Roger, General. What's the status of the PNDs? Over."

"They're safe and secure at the development center just outside of Owosso. I've just learned the move was a decoy. And for your information, that wasn't my idea. I didn't know anything about it until fifteen minutes ago."

Carl let up the accelerator, and the rig decelerated. "Smokey dead ahead," he said.

Marc took his attention off of the electronics console and stared through the windshield. A mile or so ahead, blue lights flashed on the side of the highway. "Could be Dominick's man," he said.

"Yeah," Carl replied, "and it could be the real thing. I think I need to back it down. We don't need to be wastin' time talking our way out of something."

Marc keyed the microphone again. "General, we've

got blue lights flashing on the side of the highway. We'll be checking it out. Back to you in a minute. Pathfinder clear."

Carl let the rig coast. Seconds passed, and the rig rolled to a stop near the patrol car. Now the Highway Warriors could see it. The car was wrecked, smashed into a bridge abutment. Somehow, the blue lights still revolved.

Marc was out, the silenced Uzi in his hands, the instant the rig rolled to a stop. He moved cautiously toward the smashed car. At first glance, he knew anyone unfortunate enough to be inside was dead. The car sat at an awkward angle against the giant concrete pillar. The front of the vehicle—the grille, radiator, and headlights—was now even with the windshield. The engine and transmission were sitting precariously in the front seat. And the camo-clad driver, obviously dead, lay mutilated all over the front of the passenger area.

"What's the score?" Carl asked as he walked up behind Marc.

"Take a look," Marc said. "I guess the search for this one is over."

Carl looked into the car. He turned around and faced Marc. "Damn, man, what a mess. Betcha the bastard never knew what hit him. He never had a chance."

"Neither did the people they killed when they hit the convoy," Marc said. "Somehow my heart doesn't have any room for sympathy. Let's roll. We'll get the general to call somebody to come clean up this mess."

Marc and Carl jogged back toward the rig. "Want me to drive awhile?" Marc asked.

"Sure," Carl said. "I could use a break."

Marc climbed aboard the cab on the driver's side. He fastened his seat belt and slipped into gear. The rig moved slowly forward. Then he caught another gear and gained speed.

Meanwhile, Carl lifted the Icom noise-canceling microphone and called General Rogers to bring him up-to-date on the patrol car.

Marc eased the rig up to one hundred miles per hour. The machine handled beautifully. The advanced-design integral drag foil caused the slipstream to glide easily over the trailer and reduced wind resistance drastically. The giant power plant—fourteen hundred horsepower of custom diesel—made high speeds simple. "Exit coming up ahead. I'm going to keep it down and rely on the ODS to keep us rolling safely. I suspect we'll find more traffic after we pass the exit," Marc said.

Carl worked the keyboard for the on-board multitasking computer. In less than a second, the detailed topographical map of Michigan reappeared. The weapons-system control window jumped to the left corner of the screen and remained there in reduced form. "What's your gut telling you on the path these guys will take?"

Marc watched the highway carefully. There was no traffic so far, and that was good. It also stood to reason that the speeding tanker could run just so fast if traffic picked up. Dominick and company were fleeing for their lives, and surely whoever was driving wouldn't run the risk of an accident that would slow them down. "It's anybody's guess. I think they're in too deep to bail out of the program now. My hunch is either Owosso or that place called the Dunes over on the shore of Lake Michigan. They still have the launchers, some of the PNDs, and enough plutonium to build more. They aren't carrying the things around with them, so they must have them stashed somewhere. We have some serious questions to answer before we can stop Dominick's madness. Where are they hiding the devices and the plutonium? Do they have the technology necessary to build more devices? And more importantly, what's Dominick planning to do with them?"

"I wish I could answer that," Carl said. "I just know

one thing for sure. If Dominick or some of his crazies detonate any of those PNDs, accidently or on purpose, and this arctic blast keeps drifting south throughout the country, the midwestern United States is in for some serious troubles."

Marc nodded in agreement. "We can't let that happen . . . no matter what it takes."

Andy Starr dropped his speed back to seventy-five after he passed the exit. Traffic had built up now with late-night commuters traveling the interstate. He hadn't spoken since the crash minutes earlier. Dave Craft had been a trusted, loyal solider in the mercenary legion. Even Starr thought there was something almost irreverent in his death. It simply wasn't fitting for a man of the gun to die in an accident. And for that Starr was sorry.

Dominick was completely silent also. The look of horror he had seen frozen across Craft's face in the final second of his life would remain etched in his mind forever. There had been an unspoken communication between the two men in that instant when their eyes locked. Craft's eyes were filled with disbelief and Dominick's with a plea for forgiveness. In Dominick's case, although he was a confirmed hardcase, he still possessed a streak of humanity where people of his own kind were concerned.

Starr wove the rig through the traffic. He glanced at Dominick. "Get over it," he said. "It was a mistake. It couldn't be helped. He was in the wrong place at the wrong time."

"That doesn't make it any less painful," Dominick said. "Killing someone who stands in the way of a mission is one thing. Killing one of our own by mistake is something else again."

"Look at it this way," Starr said. "Maybe it helped settle the differences between you and me. If we're going to finish this thing and make the deal with Shirnade, you and I had better settle everything between us. I say we drop whatever happened tonight and go from there. We need a plan, or that Mideast maniac will do anything it takes to hunt us down and kill us like dogs."

"Yeah," Dominick said. "I guess what happened a while ago was just nerves. Let's let the whole thing drop. The way I see it, we've got to get some other form of transportation. As soon as a cop or the security troops get to that mess we left at the northbound barricades, we'll have everyone in the country with a gun looking for us. What do you think?"

"You're right," Starr agreed. "We need another ride."

"Any ideas?" Dominick asked.

Starr gazed out at the highway and taillights in front of the tanker. His headlights fell upon a sign at the side of the road: REST AREA—1 MILE. "Yeah, I do have an idea." He slowed the rig and moved into the right lane. When the rest-area exit appeared, he turned onto the ramp and tapped the brakes.

"What's the plan?" Dominick asked as the rig rolled to a stop in the truck parking area. At least a dozen eighteen-wheelers were parked there. Some had their engines idling, and others were shut down. A service building sat opposite the truck parking area. On the other side of the service building, a large paved lot provided parking for cars.

"We sit tight and watch the place for a few minutes. See what's moving and where the sleepers are. Looks to me like we have our choice—we can take a car or another truck. What's your pleasure?"

Dominick scanned the area. There were a few people moving from the rest rooms to the parking lots. He suspected many of the truck drivers were sleeping, and if they were, he and Starr could take their pick of the unsuspecting victims. "I'm with you. Let's sit on it a few minutes and see what evolves. I don't think we have much time to waste, though. Headhunters are surely rolling, and they'll be looking in every crevice along this highway."

"Let's be logical about this. A big truck would be harder to stop, but a car is certainly faster and less conspicuous. What do you think?"

Dominick looked around nervously. "The more distance we can put between us and the attack area in the least possible time, the better. I say we take a car. Preferably a new one."

"Makes sense to me," Starr replied.

Dominick looked hard at him. "How are you going to get to the car parking lot on the other side of that building without every living soul out there seeing our weapons? We can't leave them, and the last thing we need is to attract attention to our new ride."

"We'll just have to keep them low by our legs and stay in the shadows as much as possible. If we play it cool, no one will pay any attention to us. You've got to figure everyone out here at this hour is tired anyway. They're not likely to be very alert."

"I don't like it," Dominick said.

"Neither do I," Starr replied, "but it's a chance we'll have to take if we want a car. If we're cautious, I think we can make it without much trouble."

Dominick stroked his cheek and stared out the windshield. "Okay. I don't see many other options."

Starr checked his waistline holster for the Beretta 92 he had tucked away there. He shifted his camo jacket to cover the grips of the gun and opened the door. "I'll leave the AK here and make a recon run. You stay put and keep your eyes open. If you see anything suspicious, get this thing rolling. Don't worry about me—I'll catch up to you somehow. If it goes smoothly, I'll be back in a few minutes."

Dominick nodded and shifted the muzzle of the AK across his lap.

Starr climbed from the cab and walked nonchalantly across the lot to the service building men's room. Once inside, he found a vacant urinal and relieved himself. He went back outside in front of the building, facing the parking area for cars where at least two dozen were parked. People were milling around, stretching, or walking to or from the rest rooms. Starr stood there for two or three minutes. He stretched and yawned in an effort to fit into the crowd. While he did that, he scoured the cars one by one. Nothing looked particularly inviting, so he waited.

The sound of a helicopter approaching over the truck parking area distracted him. Starr tried to appear unconcerned but knew it wasn't working. He moved to the back side of the building near the truck lot.

Then he saw it. The chopper came in low from the west and made a pass over the parking area. It banked hard right, circled, and made another pass. This time it swooped lower and hovered for a long moment before banking another hard right and disappearing into the darkness.

Starr stayed close to the rear wall of the building. He still tried to look unconcerned, but the chopper had captured the attention of every person in the rest area. Starr watched the crowd.

A low rumble rolled through the crowd as everyone talked at the same time. Starr stayed quiet. He looked into the darkness and waited nervously to see if the helicopter made another pass.

Tommy Dominick leaned toward the windshield to get a look at the chopper. He couldn't see it, but he felt the vibrations from the downdraft created by the rotors. The rig shook as the huge Cobra gunship hovered overhead. Dominick didn't know what to do. He felt chill bumps run up his spine and along his arms. He tried to convince himself that the appearance of the chopper was just coincidence, but he knew that wasn't true. They were searching for the rig, for him and Andy Starr.

The rumble of the chopper's engine rocked the parking area when the gunship reappeared out of the darkness. For a second, it seemed to hang like a monster dragonfly in the night sky, ominous and deadly. Then the parking lot was lit with the intensity of daylight as a portable sun came on beneath the mighty machine. The warship moved slightly forward and hovered near Tommy Dominick and the stolen tanker. The rotor draft whisked through the lot, and the tanker rocked again.

Dominick moved feverishly into the driver's seat. He checked the AK to be sure there was a round in the chamber. There was. He leaned forward and looked skyward. The undercarriage of the big warship was visible, but he couldn't tell much about it because of the blinding light. He jerked back in the seat and felt his blood pressure rising. He was breathing hard and on the brink of total panic. His first thoughts were that this couldn't be happening. Everything, from the theft of the PNDs to the heist of the plutonium, had been meticulously planned in infinite detail. But now he knew that somehow everything had gone astray.

Suddenly the night came alive with the sound of a firm, disciplined voice blaring over a public-address system. It came from beneath the chopper and rolled over the area louder than the rotor and engine noise. "You in the Trans Continental tanker. You have no way to escape. This is the United States Army. Throw your weapons from the vehicle and step into the light."

Dominick froze.

The voice blared again. "Thomas Dominick, we are giving you ample warning. We are under orders to open fire if you do not surrender immediately. You and your accomplices must throw out your weapons and step out of the tanker now!"

Over by the building, Andy Starr's eyes widened, then lit up. If the men in the chopper thought Dominick's accomplices were in the the truck, he realized he had a chance to escape. He turned his attention to the crowd and searched each face. He decided to move to the other side of the building and check the car parking area one more time. He turned his back on Dominick and the truck, and quickly walked away.

Dominick was frantic. Thoughts raced through his mind so fast, he couldn't comprehend them. He looked at Starr's AK lying in the space between the driver's and passenger seats. He lifted and cradled it after laying his own weapon across his lap. Logic dictated that he couldn't outrun the chopper in the rig. And Starr was still somewhere near the building across the parking lot. He couldn't leave him—not so much out of loyalty but because two blazing guns and two shooters were better than one in a contest for survival, especially against superior firepower.

Dominick looked across the lot and searched for any cover he could use if he made a run for the safety of the building. Surely, he decided, the military wouldn't open fire on an area where there were innocent civilians, no matter how badly they wanted him. Then he formulated a plan.

Andy Starr searched the car parking area again, and walked toward the cars parked there. The few people who were left were moving quickly toward the back of the building to see what the commotion was about. Starr walked down the sidewalk, casually surveying each car. He tried not to attract attention to himself. He spotted a gray Cadillac at the end of a row. His eyes locked on the driver, and he moved toward him.

The PA speaker blared again. "Dominick, last call.

Shut the engine off and exit the vehicle. You have ten seconds. Then we will open fire."

Dominick looked through the windshield once more. The helicopter had moved directly overhead now. It hovered there, ready to rain death on the tanker. He moved quickly and lowered the AK across his lap beside the other one. Then he depressed the clutch, released the parking brake, and dropped the rig into gear. In one smooth motion, he eased out on the clutch, and floored the accelerator.

The tanker lurched forward, and diesel smoke poured from its stacks. Dominick drove the rig straight across the parking lot and aimed for the center of another tanker a hundred yards away. He steered with one hand and pushed the door open with the other.

The chopper moved with him. Words he couldn't understand blared from the PA speaker. When he was thirty yards from the other tanker, Dominick changed gears, closed his eyes, and held the accelerator to the floor.

Machine-gun fire peppered the pavement around the Trans Continental tanker and sent chunks of pavement and dirt sailing into the air. The debris slapped into the rig like a savage hailstorm, but Dominick was undaunted. He waited until the rig was ten yards from the parked tanker, then leapt from the door. He hit the ground hard, dropping one of the AKs. He reached back and retrieved it as he came out of a roll. He ran ten feet to a parked flatbed rig and rolled beneath it.

The chopper pilot moved the warbird back and forth, searching for Dominick and anticipating the impact.

It came.

A crashing thud and the sound of metal tearing into metal echoed across the parking area. Sparks flew for an instant, and then the parked tanker collapsed in the middle from the impact of the speeding runaway rig.

Dominick came out on the far side of the flatbed. His AK was shouldered, his finger on the trigger. He unleashed a long burst into the underside of the helicopter. Suddenly there was darkness again when his 7.62 x 39mm scorchers penetrated the safety-glass globe of the portable sun.

The chopper pilot was stunned for just an instant as the chopper hovered over the impact area, then entered a swooping bank maneuver to come around and sweep the area again.

Dominick tapped out another staccato of death from the AK, but it wasn't needed.

The night once more became bright, but this time it came from the fiery explosion of the tankers. A giant fire-ball spiraled into the night sky as a sea of flame enveloped the parking area.

Tommy Dominick was on his feet running toward the service building before the fire scoured the pavement beneath the flatbed. He glanced over his shoulder as another massive explosion shook the ground beneath his feet. He jerked his head back to the front and ran harder than he had ever run in his life. He knew he had to find Andy Starr if either of them was to survive.

Chapter Nine

Marc watched the highway carefully. He jerked fully alert when he saw a reddish-orange cast appear on the horizon. "Hey, bro, unless I'm seeing things, I'd say there's trouble ahead. Take a look."

Carl looked up from the electronic console and peered into the dark Michigan night. "Yeah, looks like a big fire out there. You don't reckon?"

"Who else?" Marc replied.

"Could be a factory or something. Night skies play strange tricks sometimes. You know that."

"I guess we'll know soon enough. It doesn't look to be more than five or six miles away. Scroll the map and see what comes up."

"Scrolling," Carl replied. He focused back on the computer screen and enlarged small sections of the full-color topographical map until he had the section he wanted. He examined the detail closely. "Looks like there's a rest area up that way. Could be in the general vicinity."

"That would make sense—or would it?"

"What do you mean?" Carl asked.

"Would you stop at a rest area if you were on the run? Especially one so close to the scene of your crime?"

"You've got a point. My gut tells me we aren't dealing

with people who do anything logically. If they stopped, they had to have a damn good reason. You can bet they weren't looking for the men's room," Carl said as he watched the computer screen.

"Could society be so lucky as to have those slimebags involved in a fiery wreck?"

"Sounds like a fitting end to me," Carl quipped.

General Rogers's voice crackling from the Icom speaker broke the conversation. "Pathfinder, this is Barnburner. How copy?"

"Go, General," Carl said as he keyed the microphone.

Rogers spoke quickly, excitement in his voice. "Men, I just got word that an intelligence-recon gunship has Dominick's stolen tractor-trailer spotted and cornered at a rest area. I'm watching you on the satellite tracking beacon, and your signal is coming from four and one-half miles from the coordinates given by the ship's navigator a minute or two ago. Can you close into that area and give them a hand?"

"Affirmative, sir," Carl replied. "Is the gunship positive of the identification?"

"Affirmative, Pathfinder. It's a Trans Continental tank truck. Our people gave out the description just a few minutes after you left the scene where the driver was killed. Now, there is one more major glitch to this fiasco."

"What's that, sir?" Carl asked.

"We have gotten preliminary information to indicate that truck is hauling concentrated potassium cyanide. It's highly volatile and extremely deadly. If that tank should somehow rupture, the vapors alone are incredibly lethal. My people here say it would only take a minute dosage to cause virtually instantaneous death. If you're going in there, please exercise extreme caution. A stray bullet could send that stuff into the air, and we would have a very fragile situation on our hands. Do you copy? Over."

"Wonderful," Marc mumbled. "That's just what we don't need."

"Affirmative, General. We copy just fine," Carl said. "What is the designated method of handling those chemicals?"

"I'm checking on that now. If a spill occurs, we will have to do major evacuations. In concentrated form, just the vapors from potassium cyanide can create fatal conditions for miles if it gets caught on the right wind. That would not only be catastrophic—it would open the door to some sensitive questions. Those are questions the president would rather not address just now. Do you follow me, Major?" Rogers asked.

Carl hesitated for a few seconds, then answered, "Affirmative, sir. We'll do our best to separate Dominick and his companion from the rig without compromising its integrity. General, we see a luminous halo in that direction. It seems to be hanging on the horizon. We were discussing it when you called. If you have radio contact with the helicopter, could you get us a status report? If that tank is on fire, we need to know it before we go storming into the area. Over."

"Roger, Major. I have a communications technician trying to make that contact now. I've also taken the liberty of contacting the Boss on the situation. He is forwarding the status directly to the powers that be at the Environmental Protection Agency and Federal Emergency Management Agency. That's a precautionary measure, you understand."

"Understood, sir. We'll stand by on the frequency until we get word back from your chopper pilot," Carl said. He lowered the microphone and stared at Marc. "How do you fight something like this, bro?"

Marc increased their speed. He watched the broken white centerline on the highway go by in a continuous streak and kept his eyes firmly on the highway far ahead of the rig. "You don't. That's the trademark of a survivor. You know when to go in with hardware blazing and when to find another way. If that tank is in jeopardy, we've got to find an alternate solution."

"Yeah, but if that tank goes, maybe Dominick and friend will go with it," Carl said.

Marc smiled into the darkness. The glow on the horizon grew more intense as the rig neared its source. "If we're lucky, maybe they're already gone."

Omid Shirnade eased the rented van toward the border crossing between Canada and the United States on the east end of Detroit near Windsor, Ontario. At the end of the traffic line a half mile ahead, U. S. Customs officials moved slowly and deliberately as they examined each vehicle approaching the border. Where necessary, the officials demanded and examined passports. For most, however, it was the usual questions, basically "Who are you?" "Why are you coming here?" and "How long do you plan to stay?"

Shirnade knew the drill well. He had made the trip at this and similar border crossings many times in the past few years. Sometimes he would cross from Mexico when he was trading Russian-made fully automatic AK-47s for something valuable to his cause in the Middle East. Despite that, his personal choice was always Canada. He would normally fly into Ontario, rent a car, drive into the United States, transact his business, arrange transportation out of the country for his wares, then simply drive back into Ontario for a departing flight. The system was flawless and inconspicuous. He never carried anything that would bring attention to himself. That was a cardinal rule, one that must never be broken.

As far as customs officials in Canada or the United States were concerned, he was a Middle East businessman on a company-sponsored trip. He always took great care to ensure that his beard was neatly trimmed and his rich coal-black hair fashioned just so. That way, he fit into the pompous American crowd like any other immigrant. And his English was not only flawless, but probably better than the average American's. He had taken great pains to learn not only the language but the various regional inflections common to various parts of the country. He could play the role of a Northern factory worker or a small-town Southern farmer. That, coupled with his reputation for steel nerves, made him the ideal choice to execute illegal transactions on American soil.

Shirnade inched the van forward as the border guards cleared one vehicle after another. He wasn't especially nervous, but he did feel edgy, uncomfortable. He attributed that in part to the unexpected midsummer arctic cold front that had swooped into Michigan. He wasn't accustomed to the cold, despite his many trips to Canada. He had found in the past that by the time he had become acclimated to the chilly temperatures, he was off again to his homeland across the Atlantic. And tonight, he hoped, would prove no different.

The heater distributed warm air throughout the empty van, but even with that, Shirnade felt slightly chilled. He hoped that when he cleared the border and got the van rolling on the American highway, the air would circulate more vigorously and the chill would go away.

Five cars remained in front of him. He stayed calm and prepared the necessary paperwork for the border guard. The worst case, he estimated, would be ten to fifteen minutes before he was moving on the Michigan highway toward his meeting with Tommy Dominick later in the day.

He ran the orders of the day through his mind. First, he would rendezvous with the other people loyal to his legion and make the necessary travel arrangements for smuggling the stolen military hardware out of the United States. He would also receive the weapons necessary to protect himself in the barbaric United States. Then he would venture to the meeting place determined two weeks earlier, the place called the Dunes. Along the way, he would meet with Caroline Capenski, illegal Polish immigrant, sympathizer with the plight of his native land, and freelance spy. She, as his liaison, would travel with him to the Dunes, assist in his cover, and assure the transaction went according to plan.

He looked forward to seeing her again. She was a terrific lover as well as an extremely competent intelligence agent. Their time together always resulted in beautiful memories—and an occasional backache. Unlike the women of his homeland, she was passionate and earnest when they made love. She made him feel good, not guilty like the women at home. When they lay together in each other's arms, it was a feeling unlike any he had known with any other woman. She was moist and warm, but more importantly, she was always eager and willing to please him and herself. Maybe it was her sensuousness or the vigor with which she made love. He didn't know and he didn't care. Their bodies fit. And more times than not, when he left her, he wished their lifestyles and ideologies also fit. Unfortunately, they didn't, so theirs was an entangling relationship destined for a few precious moments stolen under the guise of duty and loyalty to their employers.

Once he arrived at the Dunes, he would insist that the hardware be inspected, then arrange payment through the mutually agreed-upon New Zealand bank for the remaining balance on the transaction's account. And depending upon the attitude and effectiveness of Tommy Dominick, he would then decide whether to save him for more dealings or terminate him to guarantee his silence. Either way, he would have the PNDs and enough plutonium to make more. And once he had them, his comrades could make war in a way their enemies would never forget.

Only one car remained in front of him now. Shirnade glanced at his watch. If he could get through the border crossing and drive quickly, he could reach Caroline well before daylight. And that would give them both ample time for proper greetings before they had to depart for the meeting with Dominick. Just the thought of it excited him.

The car in front moved, and Shirnade let the van coast to the guard shack. He stopped and rolled the window down. The guard approached, and he handed him his passport.

The guard opened it and looked at it carefully. "One moment, Mr. Shirnade," he said, then turned and walked back inside the shack.

Shirnade tried to remain calm. This wasn't normal. And if it wasn't normal, there was a reason for it. He sat as patiently as he could and prepared a plan.

The guard returned, and with him came two heavily armed Border Patrol officers. "Mr. Shirnade, please step out of your vehicle." The guard's voice was firm and emotionless.

"Sir," Shirnade said in his best English, "is there some sort of problem?"

"Just a routine check, Mr. Shirnade," said the guard, "nothing unusual. We must search your vehicle before you are permitted to cross into the United States."

"Very well," Shirnade said. "If you must, you must."

"Thank you. Now, will you please step to the curb. These two gentlemen will escort you inside and make you as comfortable as possible while our men search your van."

"Will this take long?" Shirnade asked.

"If everything is in order, Mr. Shirnade, it shouldn't take too long at all. Now, sir, would you please accompany these gentlemen inside."

Shirnade stepped from the van and joined the armed Border Patrol officers who stood there stone-faced. And at that moment, he knew Caroline would have to wait. More importantly, he wondered, what had called attention to him and the van?

Marc could see the distant sky glowing red. Whatever the source, it was an intense, raging fire. Above the flaming tongues that licked into the night, there was a tower of churning smoke that funneled upward and drifted away into the atmosphere. "If that's the rest area, the place must be an inferno. Hell's opened the gates from the looks of things," he said.

Carl stared at the glowing horizon. His mind scrolled through memories of battles fought before, and of battles yet to be won in the name of justice. "We've been to hell before, bro, but the devil was never dealing potassium cyanide. If that tanker's involved in the fire, we're in for some serious troubles."

"We should be getting some word back from Delta Command. I wonder what's taking him so long?" Marc asked.

"If the chopper's in the heat of things over there, that pilot probably has his hands full. Chopper doesn't do too well with updrafts like that. If the flyboy ain't real good, the devil could reach up from the fire and grab him. Nothing personal against the old boy at the stick over there, but I'm glad it's him and not me."

Marc let up the accelerator and allowed the Leeco rig to slow naturally. He watched the highway carefully now. Drivers were beginning to stop on the side of the road and gawk at the shooting flames. The rig slowed to forty-five. Marc watched for an opening along the shoulder and steered into the edge of the grass in the emergency lane. He stopped and watched the fire. "Give the General a few more seconds. If we don't hear from him, give him a yell on ComSat. It'd be foolish to roll right into that rest area, knowing what potassium cyanide can do. We get our lungs full and fall over dead, we aren't going to be any use to anyone but an undertaker."

Carl nodded. "It'll come soon enough. No sense rushing the inevitable, especially when you know it's in the darkness waiting for you and there's no escape. From what I remember about potassium cyanide from our training, the stuff is silent. You breathe it, and you're dead in minutes. It's quick and very, very effective. Judging from the smoke trail, we've got the wind on our side, anyway. It's blowing to the northwest. Must be a localized spiral tail coming off that arctic front."

"Let's hope it lasts," Marc said. "If the tanker is involved and that stuff's in the air, a shift in the winds could bring sudden death to everything that breathes for miles around. I'd just as soon not end up as some statistic on the evening news."

The Icom speaker rattled with the voice of General Rogers. "Pathfinder, this is Barnburner. We have lost contact with the helicopter. There is another one en route to the last known location of the gunship that had the tanker under observation. Last word we got from the pilot said the tanker was moving. There has been no further contact since then. We don't know if he's down to make the capture or if he's immobilized. Over."

"Damn!" said Marc.

Carl keyed the microphone. "General, is there any word on the integrity of the tanker? Over."

"Negative, Pathfinder. Last word was just that the rig was rolling. Nothing at all since then."

"Sure puts us in a hell of a bind," Marc said. "Pass me the mike."

Carl handed the Icom microphone to Marc. Marc

keyed it. "General, is there any information anywhere that you can lay your hands on that would give us a penetrability factor on this stuff? Over."

"I'm afraid I don't understand, Marc. 'Penetrability' in what respect?"

"We have a pair of Scott airpacks in the utility storage on the rig. If EPA or FEMA can give us a go, we'll move in over there. We need to know if the airpacks are sufficient to keep us from inhaling the potassium cyanide in the event we are exposed to it. Can you get us that information quickly?"

Rogers's voice crackled from the speaker across the ComSat-D satellite link. "The call is being made as we speak. We'll have an answer for you very soon."

"Roger," Marc said. "We're waiting."

Carl looked hard at Marc. "I know what you're thinking. You're thinking we're gonna put those tanks and masks on and go in there. Damn the potassium cyanide, right?"

"Right," Marc said quickly.

"It's shit like this that's gonna get our butts killed one of these days. You know that, don't you?"

"We're all going to die from something. It might as well be trying to wipe a little more slime from society," Marc said. He gazed at the fire and wondered if this would indeed be the last battle in the never-ending war.

"Pathfinder, this is Barnburner. Affirmative on the airpacks. Emergency management advises the packs, if worn properly, will make exposure to the vapors of potassium cyanide tolerable. They advise that you stay there no longer than necessary. Also, if you have some Vaseline on board, they advise you to line the rim of the face mask with it rather heavily. Once the mask is in position, don't move it or take it off. The petroleum jelly will help act as a seal against outside air. Is that clear? Over."

"Affirmative, Barnburner," Marc said.

"Before you leap into this, Marc, the OEM also advises you to shower with the system still in place just as soon as possible after you exit the exposed area. Your clothing should be destroyed, and everything you carry must be cleaned. The vapors apparently cling to anything they come into contact with. OEM further states that potassium cyanide is one of the deadliest of all chemicals. If that tank is ruptured, men, do not take any chances that would produce diminishing returns. I'd rather have both of you out of there safely than capture a dozen Tommy Dominicks. Besides, if he's still in the area and the tank is compromised, he's no longer a problem to us. Is that perfectly clear?"

"Affirmative, Barnburner," Marc said.

"Damn it, Marc Lee, no heroics. And that, Colonel, is an order. Do you copy that?"

"Roger, General," Marc said. "We'll talk with you as soon as we determine what is going on at the rest area. If something goes astray, we'll see you in hell. Pathfinder clear."

"What's your plan?" Carl asked.

"Let's get in the trailer and suit up. We can go in wearing the black jumpsuits. They're easily disposable and easy to get off. We'll follow the instructions for the airpacks to the letter. There's some Vaseline in the medicine chest back there. I figure we get ready, set and seal the masks, then get back into the rig and take a short ride. Do you see any holes in that?"

"Just a couple," Carl said.

"What's that?"

"The ones in our heads for even thinking about doing this. You realize—one slip of the mask, if the tank is ruptured, and we're dead men?" Carl said.

"Yes, I realize that," Marc said. "You're as bad as the general. You and I can count the times we've stared death straight in the eyes and lived to talk about it. It's attitude, remember?"

"Yeah, I remember," Carl replied. "I hope we know what we're doing."

"I know what we're doing, and so do you. We're going into hell to steal a couple of the devil's best. And if they're there and they aren't already dead, we're gonna kick some butt."

Carl glanced once more at the raging inferno that lit the Michigan sky. He stared for a long moment at the scorching flames. "Yeah, you're right. I'll tell you something. That sure looks mighty nasty over there. Problem is, if that tanker *has* been compromised, the biggest killer of all is the one we can't even see. Guess we'd better get suited up and go see what the devil has in store for us, huh?"

"Yeah," Marc said. "That looks bad, all right, and the potassium cyanide is an invisible killer. The worst part is, all the destruction and death that tanker and its cargo is capable of inflicting can't hold a candle to the destructiveness of even one of the stolen personal nuclear devices. And that, my friend, is what we have to stop. No matter what the cost."

Chapter Ten

□ □ □

The first explosion caused both tankers to rock. The tanker struck by Dominick's runaway machine erupted into a massive fireball when two thousand gallons of volatile gasoline ignited with a hellish fury. The second explosion followed within seconds and sent another torrential fireball rolling skyward. This one bore a danger far beyond the savagely fatal hellfire, for on its wings the killer vapors of potassium cyanide permeated the air. The silent deadly vapors rolled high into the sky from the force of the explosion, and the winds sent a quiet merchant of death across the Michigan darkness.

The Cobra pilot reacted as quickly as his body allowed. He jerked hard on the stick at the first sight of fire on the ground beneath him. His reactions were far too slow, and his machine responded much too late. The pillar of fire slammed into the underside of the aircraft with an intensity equal to a moderate tornado. The scorching winds tore through the rotors and created radical instability. In an instant the aircraft became a superheated death trap from which there was no escape. Despite the pilot's proper responses, the machine did not respond under the force of the blast. It was engulfed in fire, and then the fuel tanks ruptured. The chopper disintegrated the second the high-octane aviation gasoline met the roaring flames. Fiery chunks of the aircraft sailed in erratic directions and plummeted to the parking area below.

Fires were raging now in every corner of the parking lot. When the flaming wreckage of the devastated rigs and the helicopter landed atop the rigs parked in the lot, the torrent of hellfire multiplied.

Truckers who were sleeping in their rigs died almost instantly from the combination of concentrated potassium cyanide and intense heat. The parking lot was now a hellground with no gates, no exit. Those unfortunate innocents who were trapped there died horrid, unnecessary deaths, albeit fast ones. Most died before they even awakened to what had killed them.

Tommy Dominick reached the back of the service building. A frightened crowd scattered before him as he ran for safety. A trucker stepped into his path and tried to tackle him, but a long burst of autofire slammed into his body, and he crashed to the ground, dead.

Dominick spun right and searched the faces looking on in horror. Andy Starr wasn't among them, so he kept running. And behind him, the spreading torrent of fire consumed yet another eighteen-wheeler. The ground rocked from the explosion when fire ate through to the fuel tanks.

Dominick was almost out of control. Besides survival, his mind was now consumed with the thought that Starr had left him in the jaws of the beast. But then he saw him. He ran hard along the sidewalk in the car parking area. Starr was almost at the end of the parking strip. He held a man around the neck, and Dominick could see the barrel of Starr's Beretta pressed firmly into the man's temple.

Dominick's vision was fading when he reached Starr and the man. He was out of breath, and his heart pounded inside his chest. He looked at the old man, then at Starr.

"We've got to get out of here. There was something in that tanker we were in. People near the parking area are dropping like flies in a Raid factory. Ditch that old codger and let's get the hell out of here while we still can."

"I've got a better idea," Starr said. He shoved the old man hard against the side of the car. Then he leaned over and opened the back door on the late-model gray Cadillac. "Get in, old man."

The old man looked up at Starr with horror-filled eyes, trembling and weak-kneed. "What are you going to do to us?"

"'Us'?" Dominick said. He leaned to the window and looked into the Cadillac. Inside sat an elderly woman. "Damn," he said. "Of all the cars on this lot you pick an old man and woman."

"Chill out, Dominick," Starr said harshly. "It's a late-model car, and these people don't look capable of causing any problems." He looked back at the old man and grabbed him by the arm. "Now get inside before I stop being a nice guy," he said.

The old man obeyed and climbed into the backseat, looking more frightened by the second. He stared into his wife's eyes as she turned in the front seat and looked toward the back.

"You look whipped," Starr said. "You can ride in the back, and I'll drive." He climbed into the driver's seat and searched for the ignition switch.

Dominick got in the back and settled in. He shuffled the muzzle of one of the AKs toward the old man and tried to relax. "Come on, man. Let's get out of here. I'm tellin' you there was something in that tanker that's lethal. Must be at least a dozen people dead behind the building. I don't know how I made it here unless the wind blew it away from me."

"Okay, okay," Starr muttered. "We're rolling." He

found the ignition and fired the engine. He dropped the transmission into reverse and backed out of the parking space. When he had straightened out, he slipped the gearshift into drive and floored the accelerator.

The Cadillac leapt forward, tires squealing. Starr steered through the maze of cars until he saw Interstate 75 in front of him. He made the final turn and straightened into the southbound lane.

The old woman in the passenger seat had not spoken. She looked totally petrified. She looked to the rear occasionally for a reassuring glance from her husband.

The old man just stared straight ahead. Finally, he spoke. "Are you going to kill us?"

"That depends entirely on how well you behave," Starr said. "We're in a hurry, and we're not in a great mood. If you two don't give us any crap, we'll let you go when we get down the highway."

"What about our car?" the old woman asked.

Starr almost laughed. "We could kill you, and you're worried about the damned car? I don't believe it."

"We worked hard and saved our money for a lot of years to buy this car," the old woman said. "It's not right that you just take it away from us."

"Hey, Tommy, you believe this?" Starr glanced into the rearview mirror toward Dominick.

Dominick just shook his head in disbelief. He looked at the old man sitting beside him. "What's your name?"

The old guy looked hard at him as if he couldn't believe what he heard. Then he answered, "Walter Steele."

"How about the old woman?" Dominick asked.

"She's my wife. Her name is Helen," Walter said.

"Well, Walter," said Dominick, "you and Helen be real nice, and we'll let you know where to find your car. We wouldn't want to keep it, you understand. We just found ourselves in a situation where we needed some immediate transportation."

Walter nodded. "Who are you?"

"Now, Walter," Starr said as he glanced into the rearview mirror again, "that's not really important. The important thing is, you two have to behave yourselves."

"Okay," Walter replied.

Helen looked at Starr, still very frightened, although somewhat reassured. "What makes young men like you pick on senior citizens like me and Walter?"

"Nothing personal, lady," Starr said. "You and the old man just happened to be in the wrong place at the wrong time."

"Exit sign," Dominick said. "We can take this road and get to where we want to go. What say?"

Starr understood that Dominick was trying to avoid saying any more than he had to in front of the old couple. Although compassion wasn't in Starr's vocabulary, he drew the line at killing kids and old people just for the sake of killing. Should it come down to the captives' knowing too much, killing them would become an entirely different matter. "Yeah, this will work," he said.

Starr slowed the Cadillac and moved into the right lane. When the ramp appeared, he exited right and rolled to the stop sign. Nothing was coming, so he sped through and entered the two-lane highway headed west. He straightened the Caddy and stomped the accelerator.

Starr's eyes caught a glimpse of the rearview mirror. And that's when he saw the blue light come on behind him. Before he could speak, a siren echoed through the night. He immediately tensed and pressed the accelerator to the floor.

Dominick shot a glance out the rear window. "Where in hell did he come from?" he shouted.

"I don't know," Starr replied quickly. "I'm not going to

stop and ask him." He gripped the steering wheel tightly and threaded the Cadillac over the narrow two-lane highway.

Behind him, the police car closed in tightly, and the bright beam of a spotlight illuminated the interior of the speeding luxury car.

"Hang on," Starr yelled. "He's going to have to run me off the road because I'm damn sure not going to stop."

The two Border Patrol officers escorted Omid Shirnade to a room deep inside the border station on the side of the highway. They directed him to a chair and ordered him to sit down.

He obeyed.

Omid retained his composure and attempted to appear more annoyed with the inconvenience of his detention than nervous. He looked around the room and found himself stunned at the bland simplicity of the surroundings. The walls were painted a dull beige, and there was only one narrow window. The only decoration was a framed color portrait of the American president. This was the first time in his many crossings at American borders that his credibility had been questioned.

He looked at one of the officers who stood by the door and read the name on the name tag above his left shirt pocket. "Excuse me, Officer Ridley, have I done something wrong?"

Ridley seemed caught off guard when Omid spoke his name. He jerked to attention and stared back at him. "To this point, Mr. Shirnade, this is a routine spot check of you and your vehicle. We do that occasionally."

"This is rather an inconvenience. If I've done nothing wrong, will I be detained for very long?" Shirnade asked pleasantly.

"If the search of your vehicle doesn't come up with

anything, you will be allowed to continue into the United States quite soon," Ridley said without emotion. "In the meantime, would you please step to that desk and empty the contents of your pockets."

The second officer moved toward the desk and stood there expectantly as Omid rose from the chair. Omid looked at his name tag. He looked at the officer and smiled when he stopped in front of the desk. He reached his hands into his pants pockets first and lifted the contents. He scattered keys and Canadian coins gently over the desktop. "Officer Basilitis, I trust it isn't a crime to carry my pocketknife into your country." Omid held the knife in his open hand for Officer Basilitis to see. "It's my favorite, an old-timer. I purchased it on a previous visit to the United States."

"No," Basilitis said. "That's not a crime. You may carry your knife with you when you leave."

"Good," Omid said, and smiled as he laid the knife on the desktop with his other belongings.

"Now, Mr. Shirnade, would you please empty the contents of your jacket pockets. We must examine them also," Officer Basilitis said.

Omid did as he was told. He laid a rental-car receipt and some Canadian paper money on the desk. Then he turned the pockets inside out and let his hands fall to his sides. "That's it, gentlemen. I have nothing else on my person except my wallet. Shall I empty that also?"

"Please," Officer Ridley said.

Omid obeyed once more. Then a knock sounded at the door. Officer Ridley opened it, and another man entered the room. He was dressed in a brown sport coat, tie, and khaki pants. He moved toward the desk, shot a nonchalant glance at the contents spread out there, then looked Shirnade directly in the eyes. "Mr. Shirnade, I am Special

Agent Joseph Lillard, of the United States Border Patrol. I'd like to ask you a few questions."

"Certainly," Omid said. "I'll try to cooperate in any way I can. I still feel as if I've broken some American law. Have I?"

No one answered.

"Mr. Shirnade," Lillard began, "what is the purpose of your visit to the United States?"

"I'm here on business for my company," Shirnade said. "I am going to examine some new products for consideration by our operations management."

"I see," Lillard said. "And how long do you plan to stay in the United States?"

"Three or four days at the most, I hope."

"And what products will you be examining while you are here, sir?" Lillard asked.

"Diamond-tipped tungsten carbide drill bits for use by our core research unit. I'm an acquisitions specialist. It's my job to know hardware. I always do personal examinations, and if I find it acceptable, then I negotiate the best possible terms for the acquisition. You will find my name on your registry of foreign representatives."

"Mr. Shirnade," Lillard said, "are you familiar with an organization called Interpol?"

"I have heard of it, yes."

"We are running a routine check of you and your identification through that organization. Is there a reason we could find anything of interest?"

"I would think not," Shirnade said. "I'm not aware of any violations. I'm a businessman on a business trip, gentlemen. I have nothing to hide from you. I am trying to enter your country for business purposes. No more, no less."

"I see," Lillard said.

"Please, gentlemen, while I find all of this very

intriguing, I am also growing further behind on my travel plans. I wouldn't want to miss my appointments."

"If we find everything in order, Mr. Shirnade, you should be able to continue your visit shortly. Please try to be patient with us," Lillard said.

"Yes, of course," Shirnade said, and he walked back to the chair and sat down.

Marc and Carl drove the Leeco rig to the entrance of the rest area. Fire raged uncontrollably everywhere they looked in the truck lot, so Marc coasted the giant machine to a stop in the car area. Both Highway Warriors looked over the area carefully through the full face masks of their Scott airpacks. What they saw nauseated them. Bodies were everywhere. Human figures littered the ground, visible in the dim lights of the rest area. As Marc and Carl moved closer to the carnage, the scene unfolded unlike anything the Warriors had seen since the hellgrounds of Nicaragua.

"My God!" Carl said. "Tell me this ain't real. Could two men possibly commit such an atrocity?"

Carl's words echoed through Marc's earpiece via the Icom U-16 radio clipped to his belt. He looked at the destruction and spoke through the mask-mounted microphone linked to the two-way radio. "This is nothing short of madness."

Carl nodded in agreement. "Remember what you said. This is nothing compared to the destructive capability of just one PND. These are madmen with no compassion for human life. We have to find them. And maybe, just maybe, they're lying dead somewhere in this holocaust."

"My gut tells me no," Marc said. "Men capable of this are cunning enough to avoid their own handiwork. Let's go check it out."

Carl took the cue and opened his door. He climbed

carefully from the rig and jumped to the ground. The silenced Uzi dangled from its sling over his right shoulder. He checked the remote pressure gauge on the Scott airpack as a final safety precaution, then moved to the front of the rig and joined Marc there. "You go left to the flank, and I'll move right. Deal?"

"Deal," Marc replied. "Keep your head down and your eyes open. Stay on channel sixteen simplex unless something major erupts. I'll make a call to the general just as soon as we scope things out."

"Affirmative," Carl said, and he gave Marc the high sign with his left thumb. "Whatever you do, bro, watch that mask. This entire area is like a giant gas chamber. FEMA is going to have its hands full with this one."

Marc returned the high sign and moved to his left toward the cars parked there. He searched them one by one and found two more bodies. Then he moved toward the rest-room building where the sidewalks were cluttered with the dead. He stopped and checked each one to confirm what he already knew. Many of the dead were lying in contorted and twisted positions, death leaving their eyes open, staring into nothingness. The killer gas knew no prejudice. It had taken young and old, male and female alike with equal vengeance.

Beyond the rest-room building, fires raged out of control. The heat was so intense, Marc had to stop and turn occasionally to avoid the burning pain. In the center of the lot lay the twisted shell of what remained of the army helicopter. The rotor blades lay bent at strange angles like a disfigured pretzel. The engine housing, ruptured and blackened, lay many yards from the rotors. And the cockpit, or at least the shell of it, lay like a giant broken jar with pieces strewn haphazardly around the lot. Eighteen-wheeler ghosts blazed columns of fire into the smoke-blackened sky.

Marc looked at it all. He saw it, but he still didn't believe it. He paused and absorbed the carnage, wondering just what country he was *really* in. What men were capable of such unconscionable madness toward another living soul? As the thought pounded into his brain, so did the answer: Tommy Dominick.

Carl moved stealthily through the shadows. He searched bodies, hoping to find at least one living person who could shed some light on the events leading up to the massive hellground. But like Marc he found only the bodies of innocents who had been destroyed by a silent and deadly thief who stole their very life under cover of darkness. The more he saw, the more he hoped he would awaken from the nightmare and discover it had all been a devilish dream. Then as he moved to the next body, he knew it was no dream. It was maddening reality that would not go away.

"How's it looking on your side?" Marc asked through the two-way radio.

"Nothing moving over here except me. Everything I see is dead," Carl replied.

"Same here," Marc said. "I think we've outlived our usefulness here. Let's make the call and get a FEMA team in here for the cleanup. Any sign of Dominick?"

"Nothing," Carl said. "All the dead over here are innocent people. Nothing to indicate anyone who would have been with Dominick. No weapons or anything like that."

"I'm switching over to the ComSat-D link. I'll meet you back at the rig," Marc said.

"Roger," Carl replied. "I'm working my way back there now."

Marc pressed the *channel-up* button on the Icom. "Barnburner, this is Pathfinder. Do you copy? Over."

Seconds passed, and then General Rogers's voice

crackled through Marc's earpiece. "Pathfinder, go with your traffic. Over."

"General, we have a hellground here. Your chopper is destroyed. We have bodies everywhere we look. Anyone who was in the vicinity is dead. The tanker is ruptured and burning. I suggest you send in a FEMA disaster team. And you're not going to be able to keep this one from the media. You'd better notify the Boss before questions start. There is no sign of Dominick. We are unable to get close enough to the tanker to tell if anyone is in it. We're going on the assumption he has escaped. Over."

"Roger, Pathfinder. I have a FEMA team rolling. Should we block the highway and evacuate the area?"

"That's the least we can do. This stuff is rolling into the sky. Winds are shifting occasionally, but they are predominantly from the southeast. This stuff is heading for central Michigan. FEMA can advise on the extent of the danger as the gases dissipate in the atmosphere. Over."

"Roger," General Rogers said. "I'll notify the Boss."

"Affirmative," Marc replied. "We're going to get away from this area and follow your instructions for cleanup. We'll monitor from the rig and call you again when we've reached a safe area. Pathfinder clear."

Chapter Eleven

The police car was ten feet behind the bumper of Starr's stolen Cadillac. The road narrowed, and the white dividing line disappeared. Now all that remained was a strip of unmarked pavement that wove its way through the flat open spaces of central Michigan. The headlights of the Caddy lit the roadway ahead, but Andy Starr still found it difficult to negotiate the sharp turns that appeared suddenly.

Helen and Walter were ghostly pale. The sharp turns bounced them from right to left like rag dolls in a windstorm.

Tommy Dominick alternated his glances between the highway in front of them and the police officer behind them. He realized he and Starr had all the odds against them. They were in an unfamiliar vehicle on unfamiliar terrain in the dark. The likelihood of escaping the officer diminished with each turn of the highway.

Starr saw the reflective letters of a stop sign shining in their headlights. The road ended and turned ninety degrees right and left. He knew he had to make a split-second decision, so he chose left. He tapped the brakes, and the Cadillac slowed slightly, skidded hard right, and fishtailed through the turn. He straightened the wheels and floored the accelerator again. The Cadillac's engine screamed from the strain as it gained speed. Starr checked the rearview mirror and saw the police car bearing down on him. The officer was unrelenting in his pursuit, his electronic siren screaming into the night.

Another turn. The Caddy skidded hard left as Starr negotiated a sharp right. This time he hit the graveled edge of the road and almost lost control. The Cadillac careened back and forth across the narrow road while Starr struggled to regain control.

He made it.

The officer closed and rammed the rear bumper of the Caddy with the front bumper of his patrol car. The jolt rocked Helen and Walter. Helen screamed and looked back at the patrol car, then turned back and faced the front. Her breathing quickened, and she felt her blood pressure skyrocket.

Starr glanced once more into the rearview mirror. He yelled at Tommy Dominick, "Get your window down and kill that crazy bastard."

Dominick found the electronic window switch. The motor inside the Caddy's door hummed, and the rear window lowered out of sight. Dominick turned the muzzle of the AK-47 toward the window and leaned out. He shifted his aim toward the front of the police car and unleashed a burst of full-auto deathfire.

The patrol car careened left, then right. The officer backed off slightly but continued the pursuit.

Dominick could see the round holes bored into the police car's windshield behind him. He pointed again and tapped out a staccato burst of five or six rounds. He was lifting the AK toward his shoulder and starting to aim when the Cadillac negotiated a hard left turn. The inertia slammed him back into the window frame. He hit his right elbow and almost lost his grip on the autogun. Dominick ducked back inside to regain his composure.

The road became a long straightaway now. Starr mashed the gas pedal all the way to the floor and held it there. The Caddy's engine strained. Starr glanced at the speedometer. The indicator was buried in the far right.

The patrol car closed on the fleeing Cadillac again as the officer heightened the pursuit. He was almost on the bumper of the Cadillac when he cut to the right and tried to get beside the fleeing car.

Starr saw it coming. He cut to the right and cut the officer off. He immediately swerved back to the left and stayed in the center of the pavement.

The officer tried the left side. He closed on the Caddy until he was even with the rear bumper, then moved to the left and tried to slam into the rear fender.

Starr cut him off again. He swerved and then began a zigzag pattern. The Cadillac sped ahead, but then out of the darkness far in front another pair of revolving blue lights appeared.

"We got trouble," Starr yelled. "Cop in front. Take that son of a bitch out back there. We've got to get rid of one of them."

Dominick leaned out the window and opened fire. He dumped the remainder of the thirty-round magazine and ducked back inside. He changed sticks and leaned out again. The patrol car was still coming on hard, although he had backed off a little. Dominick pointed the autogun and fired a long burst of 7.62 x 39mm penetrators.

A geyser of hot steam became visible in the beam of the patrol car's headlights. Dominick opened fire with another burst of scorchers, and the patrol car careened left. This time it left the roadway and hit the ditch parallel to the pavement.

The officer lost control, and the car rocketed skyward. It hit the ground and spiraled back onto the highway. The car swerved across the blacktop and hit the ditch on the opposite side. It left the ground again and rolled over and over into the darkness of a Michigan farmfield.

"All right!" Starr yelled. "One asshole down and one to go." He slammed on the brakes and slid the Cadillac to a stop. He cut the headlights and pulled off the edge of the road into the darkened field. Then he jumped from the Caddy and grabbed an AK from Dominick through the open back window. "Watch 'em while I take care of this guy." He crouched behind the Cadillac's trunk and waited for the patrol car to get into range.

The officer topped a small rise and appeared out of the darkness. He saw nothing, so he slowed somewhat and looked for the vehicles he had seen seconds earlier.

Hellfire came from the darkness and shattered the patrol car's windshield. Three lethal bullets ate through flesh and bone. The lawman was dead before he realized he was hit.

The patrol car ran crazily out of control. Like the one seconds before, it hit the ditch parallel to the road and careened wildly through the field. It found a utility pole fifty feet from the pavement and slammed into it at high speed. The crash ruptured the patrol car's battery, and sparks flew into the darkness. The sparks met fuel from the twisted gasoline line, and a roaring inferno ballooned skyward, followed a second later by a cyclonic explosion.

Helen and Walter were speechless. They watched in horror as fire devoured the remains of the police car.

Starr climbed back into the driver's seat and fastened his seat belt. "Next?" he said arrogantly as he dropped the Cadillac into gear.

"I hope you know where we are," Dominick said from the backseat.

"I do," said Starr, chuckling. "We're lost."

"Mr. Shirnade, you are free to go," Lillard said. "You may recover your belongings and continue on your way. On behalf of the United States government, I apologize for any inconvenience your detention might have caused you."

Shirnade forced a smile and walked back to the desk where the contents of his pockets were spread out. He picked up everything and deposited it into the appropriate pocket. Then he turned and smiled at Officer Ridley, who watched his every move with unconcealed suspicion. "Officer Ridley, have a pleasant day," he said as he left the room.

Lillard waited outside. He handed him the keys to the rented van. "I'll escort you to your vehicle, Mr. Shirnade."

Shirnade nodded and followed Lillard to a parking area inside a high chain link fence.

Lillard stopped and pointed to the exit. "Through the gate and to your left, and that will put you back on the highway. Enjoy your stay in the United States, and I hope your business trip is profitable."

"Yes, thank you," Shirnade said. "So do I." He opened the door to the van and climbed in, then turned the ignition switch, shifted into gear, and left the lot.

Once back on the highway, Shirnade ran through the situation. He still couldn't decide if the detention had been deliberate or if indeed it had been just a random search as the officers had said. He suspected the former. And that was not good.

Shirnade let his mind wander as he drove across Michigan backroads toward Owosso. He glanced at his watch and decided that he could still make it before daylight. He succumbed to speculation and wondered if perhaps the detention could mean something had gone astray with Dominick and, if so, what effect it would have on his plans to purchase and divert the personal nuclear devices to the Middle East. He then made a pact with himself that if indeed Dominick had done something to arouse suspicion, he would terminate him immediately upon concluding the business transaction. He had long ago learned that in international underground dealings, there was no margin for error. Any leak or unnecessary attention could not be tolerated, for seemingly insignificant occurrences had a tendency to become publicized international incidents. After all, the very heartbeat of his international action committee depended upon one thing—security.

Time passed quickly while minutes became miles. When he reached the sleepy central Michigan town of Owosso, Shirnade noticed the first fingers of daylight stretching across the eastern sky. He drove to the address where Caroline would be waiting. The maze of checkerboardlike streets wove their way through the old-money section of the quiet little town. He found the house and drove the van into the driveway. But rather than get out, he sat there for several minutes. He turned his head back and forth, checking to be sure there was no tail.

When he was satisfied, he climbed from the van and went to the front door of the old brick house. Vines of ivy clung to the walls and extended upward until they almost reached the gutters. The house was trimmed neatly in chocolate brown. Large old trees stood in the small front yard near the sidewalk. And on the ground a rich green lawn covered the earth. The sidewalk leading to the arched front door was old hand-laid red brick. Along the edges of the brick, a thin layer of gray and green moss created a border.

Shirnade stopped and rang the doorbell. The door opened, and there before him stood Caroline. She was her usual charming self. Her dark hair glistened in the first light of morning. She wore no makeup, nor did she need any. Her skin was smooth and filled with the energy of youth. She stepped back and smiled. "Come in," she said, "I've been expecting you. Problems?"

"No." He walked inside to the foyer.

"Good." Caroline said. "Would you like a cup of coffee?"

"Yes," Shirnade said. He noticed then how sheer her white nightgown was. He could see her tantalizing naked body beneath it.

"Come here first," Caroline said. "We have some time before we have to leave." She tugged on the bow that held the top of her nightgown together, then opened her arms to him. And before either of them realized what was happening, their bodies were tangled, their lips pressed against each other.

Marc had driven the rig twenty miles south of the ill-fated rest area. He found a convenient place to stop and parked. He and Carl entered the living quarters of the Leeco trailer after shedding their black jumpsuits. They stayed on the Scott airpacks, then showered exhaustively until all residue of the potassium cyanide had been washed away. When they were finished, they relaxed in their bunks and tried to get some rest.

The *alert* tone on the ComSat-D satellite link awakened them. Marc sat up and looked at his watch, then glanced at the color monitor of the closed-circuit high-definition television. Daylight outside. He slipped from the bunk and moved to the communications command console. He lifted the microphone and made the return call through the orbiting ComSat-D satellite. "Barnburner, this is Pathfinder. You have traffic?"

The voice rocked through the speaker almost the

instant Marc released the *transmit* switch. But this time it wasn't General Rogers. The voice was that of Colonel Gary Placeway at Delta Force Command deep inside the secure walls of the Pentagon. "Hey, sunshine, didn't mean to wake you. Who am I kidding, of course I did. You need to be up anyway. The good general had to go get some shut-eye, so I've got the honor of manning your control station. Where you been hiding? Haven't talked to you in a while. FEMA is commanding the cleanup at the rest area. Hell of a mess, from what I hear. Must be some real bad boys playin' around out there. Anyway, the reason I rang your chime is, I've got some more updated information for you. You awake enough to follow along or should I give you a couple of minutes to clear your head? Over."

Marc pressed the *transmit* switch. "If you talk real slow, you can go ahead while I plug in a pot of coffee. I'm coming up on uplink Charlie. If you'll downlink on Charlie and uplink Baker, we can go full duplex. I'll set the VOX and get myself a little more humanized. It was one hell of a long night. Are you ready to move to the duplex link? Over."

"Affirmative. Barnburner poppin' switches. Stand by."

Marc made the transmitter and receiver link changes on the all-mode Harris transceiver that was the heart and soul of the Leeco rig's communications center. He set the VOX to engage the voice-operated transmitter relay. When he was finished, he transmitted again, this time speaking at a comfortable level across the living quarters. "Am I on? This is Pathfinder. Do you copy VOX full duplex?"

"Bet your sweet behind, Pathfinder. Got you all the way," Placeway said.

"Great," Marc replied. "Now, what's the update? Wait, let me guess. You've already nailed Dominick, and Carl and I can go south to Alabama for a little R and R. Am I right?"

"You wish," Placeway said. "You know this game of

catch-and-kill doesn't go that way. Your quarry always plays hard to get. Something to do with dying. Now, back to business. We got a call from our man on the scene in Michigan, and it seems Michigan State Police had something interesting to tell. About the time you boys were going into the rest area, a local cop got after a gray Cadillac several miles south of where you were. They were coming off I-Seventy-five at an exit. The cop got after them for a traffic violation. Anyway, sunshine, the short version is the Caddy made a run for it and the cop chased him. It all ended up fifteen miles off the interstate with two cops killed and two police cars totaled. Both cops had been shot several times. Investigators found a trail of Commie seven point six-two by thirty-nine brass on the highway—AK shit. The license number run by the police dispatcher comes back to an elderly man from Indianapolis. Crain had some of his people make a closer check. Turns out the guy and his wife are overdue on a return trip from Michigan's U.P. Consensus here is they ran into our boys. We figure they're either dead or being held hostage. Cop called in at least four occupants in the Caddy before his ticket got punched. Am I going too fast?"

"No," Marc said. "The coffee is just going too slow. I think I'm with you so far. Is there more?"

"Yep, there's more. The newspeople are like maggots on a week-old carcass. They're looking for somebody to blame so they can have an electronic public execution. The general and the Boss said to remind you guys to watch your backside and don't get caught in the media cross fire, lest your asses be hung out to dry for mounting on some reporter's trophy wall. You got that?"

"Always," Marc said. He sipped a cup of fresh-brewed coffee and finally felt like he might be coming awake.

Carl sat on the edge of his bunk and sipped on a

steaming hot cup also, listening attentively while Placeway talked.

"Good. Now which way are you heading?"

"West," Marc said. "I have a gut feeling about this. I'm playing a hunch and following bodies, but I think I know where Dominick and his rent-a-slime are headed. Is that it for the morning report?"

"Not quite. Just to go back and touch a few bases, the foundation of this entire operation came about because of the PNDs. Now, just after two this morning, U. S. Customs and the Border Patrol detained a man trying to enter the country from Windsor, Ontario, to Detroit. His name is Omid Shirnade. A Middle Eastern kill maniac. They ran him through Interpol and turned up zip, so they let him enter the country. An hour after the guy left, Interpol discovered this character had been red-flagged. They turned a hit on him, but he was long gone. He's a detail man for a radical Middle Eastern turban-top outfit. The bastard's a fanatical terrorist specializing in weapons acquisition and disposition. He's got a trail of death that runs across three continents, and Interpol missed him on the first swoop—can you believe that?"

"After what I saw last night, Colonel, I'd believe anything. What's the latest on Omid?"

"That, unfortunately, *is* the latest. He's somewhere in the country, probably Michigan, and the brains on this end figure he just might be here to buy himself some PNDs."

"Wonderful," Marc said.

"I knew you'd like it," Colonel Placeway replied. "If you'll activate your fax on another ComSat-D freq, I'll give you a smiling eight-by-ten of Omid."

"Sure," Marc replied. He walked back to the communications console, activated a secondary receiver, and strapped the fax machine into the output. He set both units to the *on* position and spoke to Colonel Placeway. "Let your fax roll whenever you're ready, Colonel."

The fax LED *receive* indicator lit, and the thermal paper rolled across the heat head. The portrait of Omid Shirnade appeared, one fine line at a time. In a minute the complete photo was dangling from the back of the fax machine.

"Looks like one of his finer poses," Marc said when he looked at the photo of Shirnade standing in a bunker with an AK-47 across his chest. And just as Colonel Placeway had said, Shirnade was smiling.

"Yeah, well, don't let the jovial face fool you. According to the company's file on the clown, he's not only a detail arms man, he's also a killmaster with tempered steel for nerves and ice water flowing in his veins. If he's in on the game, don't underestimate him. It could cost you your lives."

"Why is it always you who brings us such good news, Colonel?" Marc asked.

"Hey, it's because I'm such a nice friendly guy and a fountain of vital information," Colonel Placeway replied.

"Yeah," Marc said. "Do you have anything else to help us start the morning off right?"

"Nope, that's it, guys. I'll be hanging around the old console if you need me. If anything else comes across the link, I'll push the magic button and ring your doorbell. Talk to you later, guys. And just for the hell of it, be careful, huh?"

"Yeah," Marc said. "You can count on it. Always." He switched the satellite link off and reset the tone alert.

"What's your gut tellin' you, bro?" said Carl as he stood from the bunk and stretched hard.

"It's tellin' me we're into something that may have some far-reaching tentacles. With the possibility of a new player in the game, it could get nasty before it gets better."

"You think Shirnade is a player?"

Marc sipped the last of his coffee from the cup and put it on the console. "I think until it's proven otherwise, we have to act as if he is. What do you think?"

"Sounds that way, doesn't it?" said Carl. "Now, how are we going to find Dominick?"

"We're going to roll these eighteen wheels to Owosso and stay on the horn for updates. Finding him will be easy. We just follow the blood and hope we can nail him before it leads us to a mushroom cloud."

"And what about Shirnade?" Carl asked.

"If he's a player and we encounter him, we'll give him a lesson in Delta Force antiterrorist methods and applications. We'll teach him and Dominick how to pay hardball. Permanently."

Chapter Twelve

□ □ □

Andy Starr was feeling a mounting fatigue. The stress alone had been enough to kill the average man, and he couldn't forget the fact that the entire mission had been a disaster. As his body grew more weary, his mind slowed, and he replayed it all. The fact that he had been set up distressed him. And since the first shot of the attack had been fired, everything he and Dominick had planned had plummeted downward in a tailspin. Every turn brought another problem.

The path they had followed was clearly marked in blood and fire. So much so that a rookie investigator could follow them and perhaps even overtake them. But inside, he knew his cunning and abilities wouldn't permit that to happen. He was a soldier, trained in the fine art of survival, proficient in the art of killing. That was his job, and his psyche was fine-tuned to the execution of his skills. But even his abilities couldn't hide the slipstream of horror left in his wake, and Starr knew that had to stop before the trail lead directly to the Dunes.

First light had come and gone. Helen and Walter had finally fallen asleep. Starr considered that a blessing. Although he never permitted himself to let his guard down, he did rest a little easier while they slept. He had driven

135

the Cadillac more than halfway across south-central Michigan. At first, he had considered going to Owosso. Then his better judgment overruled that thought, and he decided with Dominick that the best place to go would be Grand Rapids. He wove the car through the Michigan backroads until he was northwest of Owosso and then finally found a road that took them back toward Interstate 96. Starr turned the Caddy west on I-96 and headed toward Grand Rapids.

He realized decision time was forthcoming. Soon, he and Dominick would have to rid themselves of the car. Surely every lawman in the country was looking for it now. He had stopped for gasoline once during the early-morning hours. While he stopped, he chanced a telephone call to Rick Hosfelt at the cabin on Silver Lake. The best they could both estimate, Hosfelt should be able to reach the first rest area west of Grand Rapids about the same time Starr could. And there they could ditch the old man and woman, and get on with their business.

Starr glanced into the rearview mirror and looked at Tommy Dominick. He was tired, nodding off into light sleep. Walter was off in another world, his head resting against the plush velour near the top of the right rear door. He didn't snore, but he breathed heavily, and his mouth stayed open most of the time.

Dominick was in one of the waking periods between nods, and Starr spoke to him in a low, deliberate voice. "I saw a sign a few miles back. We should be nearing the rest area soon."

"Good," Dominick said. He checked his watch and looked up at the rearview mirror so he could see Starr's face. "Rick should have had enough time to get there. We can ditch these old farts and be on our way. Are we just going to leave them?"

"If they stay asleep, yes. As long as they don't know

which way we went, they're not that much of a threat," Starr said.

"They can identify us. They saw it all—those two cop cars. I don't like it," Dominick said.

"They're both scared shitless. I think they'll be so confused when they wake up, they'll have a hard time just remembering who they are and where they've been. The important thing is to get the hell away from the rest area with Rick before anybody can see us. Once we're at the Dunes, I won't be quite so concerned."

"I still don't like it," Dominick said.

"The cops and the military already know who you are. The chopper at the rest area called you by name, remember?"

Dominick was silent. "Okay," he said. "We'll do it your way."

The exit sign for the rest area appeared. Starr slowed the Cadillac and moved into the right lane. He made the exit and drifted into the rest-area parking lot. Near the end of the line of cars, he spotted Rick Hosfelt's familiar red Chevy Blazer four-by-four. He eased the Caddy to a stop at the opposite end of the parking area. He shut the engine off, slid the keys from the ignition to keep the courtesy tone from sounding, quietly opened the door, and hit the pavement.

Dominick was right behind him. They walked quickly toward the red Blazer, their AKs down by their sides to make them as inconspicuous as possible. Helen and Walter were still asleep in the car, unaware that they were now free.

Dominick and Starr walked quickly, never looking back at the Caddy. They neared the Blazer and saw Hosfelt sitting inside. When they climbed in, Hosfelt immediately slipped the Blazer into reverse and backed out of his parking spot. He dropped the gearshift into drive and sped away from the rest area.

Hosfelt looked at his two weary companions. "What the hell happened last night? It's all over the news this morning about a military convoy being ambushed. And the explosion with the cyanide . . . wow! Half of Michigan is scared out of their minds. The news said a lot of people died. What the hell did you guys do?"

Starr looked over from the front passenger seat at Hosfelt. "We got ourselves set up, that's what we did. They knew we were coming, and they were ready for us."

"Tommy, you look like you've been beaten and left for dead," Hosfelt said to the rearview mirror.

"Yeah, right. Well, I feel like it too. Any word from Shirnade?" Dominick asked.

"Nothing. We were starting to get a little worried. You know, with the stuff on the news and all. We thought maybe you guys got your asses shot off. It scared the hell out of us," Hosfelt said.

"It was close, all right," Starr said. "If the military or the police close in on us, what they saw last night is child's play compared to what we can do with the PNDs."

Hosfelt looked shocked. "You mean you'd really use those things?"

Starr's face hardened. His voice was cold and unsympathetic. "If it meant survival, I'd do it in a heartbeat."

Caroline rolled over in the bed and gently touched Shirnade's face with her soft fingertips. "We'd better get dressed, lover. We have business to attend to."

"Yes," Shirnade said. He stared at her and absorbed her beauty. Her long flowing hair draped over the pillow beside him. The softness of her fingers against his skin mellowed him and shot a bolt of lightning through him at the same time. He admired her delicately proportioned breasts protruding from the sheet with firm, erect nipples. He reached out his hand and touched them.

Caroline slid closer to him, inviting him to kiss them. Her eyes pleaded for him to come to her.

He did.

Then their bodies were entangled again, skin against skin, heart to heart. The minutes flew by as they touched, devoured each other with the heat of their passion, and made love once more. And then her body rocked beneath his, stiffened, and seconds later, relaxed unlike any other woman Shirnade had ever known.

When the fire of passion had burned away, Shirnade slipped in close beside her. He knew moments such as these were the real treasures of life. The gold, the power, the land—all of it was just a superficial way to keep score. But in his land, his world, that was the only game to play if you wanted to live. The moments with Caroline were the only salvation in his fast-paced life of kill-or-be-killed. And he savored them because she was the only woman he had ever known who was his equal—in bed or on the killing field.

"Come now, Shirnade, we must get dressed," Caroline said softly. "We have a long ride to the shores of Lake Michigan. We must not keep our supplier waiting."

"Yes." He looked at her hard. He wanted to stay there forever, but he knew he must attend to the matters that had brought him to the United States in the first place.

Caroline slipped gracefully out of the bed and walked to the bathroom, naked. She made no effort to hide her body or cover the fine lines of her suntanned skin.

Shirnade watched her every step until she disappeared behind the bathroom door. Then the sound of the shower came from the bathroom, and he rolled over in the bed and stared at the ceiling. Why, he wondered, were women like Caroline always so near to the heart and so far away from the hand? Why were there none like her in his homeland, one he could keep?

He got out of bed, walked to the entertainment console across the room, and switched on the television. It was a morning news program. Shirnade had just sat back down on the bed when the voice of the announcer caught his attention. He listened attentively and watched the videotaped footage of a holocaust outside of Saginaw on Interstate 75. Shirnade watched for a moment, then jumped from the bed and moved quickly to the bathroom. He opened the door and leaned inside. "Caroline, come quickly and see this."

"What?" She asked from the shower. "Trouble?"

Caroline stepped from the shower, water dripping from her body. She grabbed a towel from the rack beside the shower door and walked into the bedroom as she dried her hair. Then she stopped in front of the television and stared at the screen. "Damn," she said, "they know it's Dominick."

"Yes," Shirnade said. "We must hurry to complete this transaction. Then I must kill him."

The drive to Owosso had taken an hour and a half. Carl drove the high-tech Leeco rig while Marc entered data into the fiber-optic-linked on-board computer in the cab. The optic link connected the remote unit to the mini-mainframe system in the trailer behind the cab. There, the system could search its own internal data base or link to virtually any receptive system via transmissions through the ComSat-D orbiting satellite. Marc ran the system, searching for anything that might yield a lead to the whereabouts of Tommy Dominick and his hardcore band of killers. So far, the results had been less than profitable. Nothing turned up, and there had been no further word over the ComSat-D voice links.

Carl slowed the rig as they approached the main street leading through the small Michigan town. People were stirring now, and traffic moved lazily along the thoroughfare. Most of the businesses weren't open yet, the only exceptions a couple of fast-food restaurants. Carl glanced around at the buildings and the first signs of a town awakening for another day. After the rig passed the first two restaurants, he looked over at Marc. "We're getting nowhere fast. How about some breakfast?"

Marc looked up from the computer screen at the quiet little town. "Yeah, the coffee a while back woke me up, but the belly could use some nourishment. Guess we should have fixed something while we were in the quarters. What's your pleasure?"

"I don't care, as long as it's something of substance," Marc replied. "If you see something that strikes your fancy, let's do it."

"Actually, what I'd like to have is one of my grandma's breakfast specials. You remember the kind—fresh eggs, over medium, with lots of sausage fried golden brown, hot gravy, and homemade biscuits that nobody could make like Grandma. You'd throw a big slab of fresh butter in the middle of that steaming biscuit and watch it melt. Then you'd lay the dude open and smother it in sausage gravy with just the right amount of black pepper. And when you finished that, Grandma always had a couple more biscuits still warm in the oven. Pop one open and fill it with homemade apple butter. Wow! I sure miss that." Carl licked his lips.

Carl caught Marc with his guard down. He hesitated a moment and wondered why the big Warrior was thinking of his grandma so early in the morning. Especially since the trail of the latest rapist of society had cooled so dramatically. He turned in the passenger seat and stared at his partner. "At my house, we'd skip the sausage and throw on a big thick steak. And, boy, did we have some fantastic steaks back home in Texas. Lot of water over the dam since then, huh?"

"Yeah," Carl said. "Now I *am* hungry. All this talk just made it worse."

Marc searched the streets for an open restaurant. He glanced to his left, off the main street. "Doesn't appear to be much to choose from unless you want it in a paper sack."

"Got to be something somewhere," Carl said.

"You would think so," Marc replied. Then he saw it. "Hey, there's something a block over. Would you settle for Dairy Delight?"

"Doesn't look like I have much choice. We might find something if we wait a little while, but I'm ready to eat now," Carl said.

"Take her up a block and turn left. The DD should be a couple of blocks behind us. Looked like a large parking lot next to it. You should be able to get the rig in there."

Carl negotiated the left turn, went down one block, and turned left again. Two blocks later, the giant Leeco rig pulled into the vacant parking lot at the Dairy Delight.

Carl looked the place over with trained eyes before he shut the diesel engine down and removed the keys from the ignition. It was a habit developed from years of training, and sometimes it was irritating, but he had gotten used to the idea of constant security at all costs. "Nothin' but employees stirring in there, bro. Let's go get a bellyful."

"I'm ready," Marc said. He checked the positioning of his Smith & Wesson 5906 beneath his jacket and opened the door.

The Icom speaker stopped his movement. "Pathfinder, this is Barnburner," Brittin Crain said over the radio link.

Carl stopped with his door ajar. "What timing. Sometimes I think that boy is watching every move we make."

Marc nodded in agreement and reached for the microphone. He lifted it from the cradle and pressed the *talk* switch. "Barnburner, go with your traffic."

"Pathfinder, we have just received confirmation of a brand-new game. The company got a hit from a source in West Germany. We just this minute got the word. Our boy, Omid Shirnade, is definitely in the States on business. Sources reveal that he has already cut a ten-million-dollar deal with Dominick. The company thinks this is real stuff and not just under-the-table fluff. We got us a new player, guys," Crain said.

"Marvelous," Marc said as he spoke into the satellite-linked transceiver's microphone. "Any idea of when or where this transaction will take place?"

"They're working on it, and you'd better be too. We can't let this deal go down. We have to stop these maniacs before they get the goods transferred and out of the country," Crain said.

"Are you sure Shirnade can get the goods out of the country?" Marc asked.

Crain's voice became serious. "He got in, didn't he?"

"He's got a point," Carl said. "The sucker probably has a network set up in this country. I don't think he can handle it by himself. If he has the balls to come in and make the deal himself, he can sure as hell get the PNDs out."

Marc keyed the mike. "Brittin, is there any indication where Shirnade is now?"

"Negative. Last time he was seen was by Customs and Border Patrol at the Detroit crossing early this morning. That's been several hours. He could be almost anywhere in the United States by now."

"Affirmative," Carl said.

Marc let the microphone drop to his lap. "It's got to be the Dunes. Has to be. That rent-a-slime at the terminal made too much of a point of telling me about the place. If they're not in Owosso, they've got to be there."

"It's a long shot, granted," Carl said. "But right now, it's the only lead we've got."

"Brittin, get on the horn and find Jill. Send the Learjet for her and get her to Grand Rapids within the next two hours. We'll pick her up there. Also, get a satellite sweep of a place called the Dunes on the eastern shore of Lake Michigan. I'm looking for infrared image hot spots. Radiation. If you can get a detailed shot of that place from one of the birds with a watchful eye, fax it to us. I want to see what's on the ground there. Over."

"What are you onto, Marc?" Crain asked.

"Maybe nothing, but I certainly hope not. I'm playing the gut, and the gut says they're making a move somewhere in the vicinity of that place. It stands to reason, too. It's a vacation hot spot with lots of people and a constant flow of tourists. Something I learned a long time ago. Sometimes the very best way to disappear is to blend right in with the crowd."

"Affirmative. You're calling the shots on this one. I'm just the humble messenger boy. You call the numbers, and I'll play 'em. It may take a few minutes to get all of this together. I'll have to move over to the big house in the hole to get the satellite data. I'm sure Colonel Placeway or the general can handle the request. You want me to mobilize some support for you?"

"No," Marc said. "Just get Jill moving."

"What if you're wrong and it goes down someplace else?"

"Then it's my ass. I'll take full responsibility. If you get anything else before we reach the Dunes, call us immediately. In the meantime, while you're assembling the necessary data I requested, we're going to go eat breakfast."

"Breakfast?" Crain asked. "A corps of maniacs is dealing stolen nuclear weapons, and you're going to eat breakfast?"

"Roger," Marc said. "Pathfinder clear."

"You ready?" Carl asked.

"Yeah," Marc replied, and he climbed from the rig.

The Highway Warriors entered the Dairy Delight restaurant and stopped at the order counter. Carl looked at the menu and smiled at the young girl working behind the counter. "Is your breakfast as good as my grandma's?" he asked.

"I'll try to make it that way," the girl replied. "What'll you have?"

"Four eggs, over medium. Six sausage patties, biscuits and gravy, hash browns, and one of those large cups of coffee," he said, pointing to a large sixteen-ounce cup sitting near the coffeepots.

"How about you, sir?" the girl asked.

"Make mine the same, except no coffee. Instead, make it a large chocolate malt," Marc said.

"A malt?" Carl asked.

"Yeah, goes great with eggs. I've had enough coffee this morning. Anyway, I'm a sucker for a good malt."

The girl disappeared behind the counter. Marc and Carl found a comfortable seat with a view of the doors and the Leeco rig. They sat patiently until the girl returned with their orders and sat them on the table.

Carl picked up the saltshaker, doused his eggs and gravy, then exchanged it for the pepper shaker. He covered the eggs until they were almost completely hidden beneath a blanket of pepper.

"Like a little egg with your pepper, do you?" Marc quipped.

"Sometimes," Carl said.

Marc cut into his eggs and sausage. He was half through when the door opened and a very attractive young woman walked into the restaurant. Marc watched her but tried to remain inconspicuous, although he and Carl were the only other patrons in the dining area. Behind the girl was a man. He was tall, maybe six feet, and thin. He had a beard, and his thick hair was as black as coal. His face was chiseled, lean, sharp-jawed. His skin was somewhere between dark and olive, accenting his deep-set dark eyes.

Marc tore his eyes away and continued with his breakfast. For a minute, he wasn't sure if he was seeing what he thought he saw. He tried to hide his surprise by taking larger bites. He sipped on the malt and watched the couple out of the corner of his eye.

The couple walked to the counter, and the young woman chided her companion. "See, I *told* you this was a quiet place off the beaten path. Besides," she said, "it's the only game in town that's open besides fast food."

"Very well," the man said reluctantly, and ordered.

Marc looked at Carl and knew his partner in the never-ending war against crime understood. No doubt about it—before them stood Omid Shirnade. And he looked just like the fax photo. Only this time, he wasn't cradling an assault rifle. At least not one that was visible.

Chapter Thirteen

Rick Hosfelt slowed the Chevy Blazer and turned into the gravel parking lot of the old wooden-frame general store on the side of the road. He stopped in front of the gasoline pumps and shut off the engine.

Andy Starr glanced around the area and across the two-lane road at a massive field of asparagus. Satisfied, he turned around and looked at Hosfelt. "How much longer?"

"Twenty, maybe twenty-five minutes. I'll be back soon as I fill this thing up. I don't want to be short on fuel today," Hosfelt said.

Tommy Dominick nodded awake in the backseat. He rubbed his eyes and looked around. "Where are we? Why are we stopping?" he asked.

"Not far from the Dunes," Hosfelt said. "I made a pit stop to get some gas. Won't take long. Go back to sleep if you want. I'll keep an eye out."

"Sounds good to me," Dominick said, yawning. He closed his eyes and let his head drop forward until he was as comfortable as he could get without lying down.

"Do they have a bathroom here?" Starr asked.

"All the comforts of home," Hosfelt replied. "Maybe not quite as exotic, though."

Hosfelt left the Blazer and went to the pumps. He

removed the fill-spout top and started pumping gas into the four-by-four.

Starr climbed out, stretched, and went inside. The building was quite old, its exterior covered in weathered unpainted wood. Inside wasn't much better. Rows of wooden shelves stocked a quaint assortment of cellophane-packaged perishables and canned goods. Lining the top of the walls were shelves of rough-cut wood with a wide assortment of small dry goods ranging from dust-covered life preservers to fishing lures that only a fisherman could appreciate. At the back, an open-top meat cooler spanned the length of the store. And near the front, easily accessible to customers, sat an old cold-water soft-drink chest. Above the drink cooler a sign handwritten with a red felt-tip marker read: *10-cent Deposit Required on All Beverages.* Starr chuckled and walked to the girl behind the cash register. "Do you have a rest room?"

The girl, sandy-haired and probably not over seventeen or eighteen, nodded and pointed toward the left rear of the store. "Back there. Knock first. It doesn't have a lock on the door. We only got one, for men and women."

"Thanks," Starr said. He turned and walked toward the rest room.

Outside, Rick Hosfelt was still filling the tank. He alternated his glances between the fill-spout and the road. Traffic was heavy, but that wasn't unusual for a Thursday. People would flock to the Dunes to absorb the sun and enjoy their leisure time in and around the shifting sand on the shores of Lake Michigan. He looked inside the Blazer where Tommy Dominick was sleeping soundly. Then he glanced back at the roadway and saw a highway patrol car top the rise a hundred yards from the store. "Oh, shit," he mumbled aloud. He tapped on the rear window. "Dominick, wake up. Trouble."

Dominick didn't wake up; instead, he shuffled uneasily

in the backseat, jerked his his head up, then let it drop down again.

Hosfelt tried to maintain his composure. After all, there was no way the police or anyone else would know what kind of vehicle Dominick and Starr would be in.

The police car slowed, signaled to turn, and wheeled slowly into the lot.

The officer shifted into park, shut off the engine, and climbed out. He looked around the gravel lot and nodded his head at Hosfelt in friendly greeting.

Hosfelt waved and continued to pump gas.

The officer went inside, spoke to the young clerk, and went immediately to the water-filled drink cooler. He opened the flip-up lid, found a soft drink and closed the lid. He picked up a towel on top of the cooler and wiped the bottle dry. When he had opened the drink with the opener on the side of the chest, he took a huge drink. Then he breathed a sigh. "I needed that," he said to the clerk.

The officer was exchanging small talk with the clerk when Andy Starr opened the rest room door. He started out, spotted the officer, quickly ducked back inside, and closed the door. He took a second to gather himself, then opened the door again and walked out between the rows of shelves.

Starr was halfway to the front of the store when the door opened and Rick Hosfelt entered. He slowed his pace and pretended to be looking at cans of food.

Hosfelt walked to the clerk and retrieved a wad of money from his pants pocket. "Fourteen dollars and fifty-eight cents," he said. Then he handed the clerk a ten and a five.

The clerk checked the pump register and entered the amount into the cash register. The cash drawer opened, and she counted out his change. Then she closed the drawer and handed the change to Hosfelt.

"Thanks," he said as he pocketed the coins and walked to the door.

Starr followed. He nodded to the clerk on his way out and walked as casually as he could.

Starr was ten feet past the door when he heard the officer's voice behind him. "Excuse me, sir, can I speak to you a moment?"

Starr felt a rush of adrenaline crash through his body. The cop was behind him, and Starr couldn't see him. The Beretta 9mm automatic was tucked into his belt at his waist beneath the light camouflage jacket he wore. He knew all odds were against him, so he decide to play it very, very cool. He turned slowly and locked eyes with the lawman. "Yes, sir?"

The officer already had his hand positioned near his weapon, a semiautomatic pistol of some sort on a black Sam Browne belt. He approached Starr but kept a distance of several feet. "Sir, what is that bulge beneath your jacket? Are you concealing merchandise?"

Starr appeared surprised. "Merchandise? Heavens no. That's a two-way radio. Want to see it?" Starr watched the lawman's eyes and made an emergency plan. His senses came to full alert, and his muscles tensed.

"Yes, please," the officer replied.

"Sure," Starr said. He slowly moved the jacket with his right hand. Halfway through the move, he jerked hard right and pivoted. His left leg flew outward, his foot striking the officer in the chest.

The officer fell back, his balance gone. He caught himself and struggled to remain standing.

Starr was on him again, his right foot out in a snapkick that caught the lawman in the right thigh.

The highway patrolman fell back again, stumbling hard this time, reaching for his throbbing leg.

Starr spun again, his hands up now to defend against a

punch thrown by the startled officer. A solid right came from the lawman but hit Starr's forearm and glanced off. Starr threw a hard lunge punch and pivoted his forearm. His fist caught the lawman in the left cheek, and the sound of bones breaking rattled over the impact of the punch.

The lawman fell back again. Blood trickled from his mouth now, and his eyes were open wide in fear. He fought to stay standing, won, and moved hard to the left.

Starr followed. He clenched his teeth, his jaw locked rock-hard. He moved on the lawman, and his hands moved at lightning speed in front of him like the interlocking teeth of a chainsaw. He hit the officer in the face. Once. Twice. Another blow, and a right-left combination.

The lawman's legs weakened, and he started toward the ground, but then his feet swiveled in the loose gravel and he came up spinning and kicking. His flying left leg caught Starr at the calf and knocked his legs from under him. He hit the gravel. He looked up as the officer was reaching for his weapon.

Starr spun on the ground, and his legs flew forward wildly. His left foot hit the lawman in the shin and sent him reeling backward. Starr swiveled and came up with the motion. He was on his feet again, now, and he came around with another pivoting roundhouse kick. This one caught the battered lawman on the side of the face and knocked him to the ground. Starr flipped his jacket back with his right hand and moved for the Beretta 9mm. His hand locked around the synthetic grips, and he came upward to release the weapon from the holster.

He wasn't fast enough. The officer had quickly recovered, and he moved with flying feet once again. He hit Starr on the calf for the second time and sent him reeling. Then he stepped back and drew the automatic pistol from its holster. He leveled it on Starr.

A loud shot rang out. Then another.

The lawman flinched and fell toward the ground, his pistol gone from his hands. A spot of bright red blood appeared on his upper chest, near the collarbone.

Starr was up, his eyes darting to his left. Rick Hosfelt stood in a firm Weaver stance, the muzzle of his revolver pointed at the fallen lawman.

Starr was still dazed, but he got to his feet and stumbled to the Blazer. He climbed in, and Hosfelt followed. Hosfelt fired the engine and dropped the Blazer into gear. Gravel flew in his wake as he floored the accelerator and spun out of the parking lot onto a country road perpendicular to the main road.

Shots came from behind him. The police officer was still alive. He was up and pelting hot lead into the Chevy. The officer stumbled but made it to his car. The lawman fired his engine, and the partol car surged backward. It stopped abruptly, then moved forward in a hailstorm of flying gravel.

Now there was more gunfire as Hosfelt turned onto the main road and headed for the Dunes.

The officer tried to straighten his car, but he couldn't.

Bullets from Tommy Dominick's AK-47 ravaged the patrol car. A lone 7.62 x 39mm projectile found its way through the windshield and into the lawman's face. His muscles, in their death throes, tensed and caused the accelerator to stay floored. The patrol car careened wildly and slammed into the gasoline pumps in front of the store amid another barrage of deathfire from Tommy Dominick. On impact, the gasoline pump was knocked from its stand. It sailed into the air and landed across the lot. Sparks from the crash of metal against metal met with gasoline pouring from the ruptured lines. A flash fire burst out of the melee and erupted into a mighty fireball.

The patrol car flipped over on its side while the fireball scoured the graveled lot in front of the store. Then the vicious ball of flaming petroleum vapors hit the front of the wooden structure with the intensity of a tornado. In less than the time it took to cover the front of the store, the building was engulfed in raging fire.

Hosfelt floored the accelerator. He glanced at the hellground as the Chevy sped past it. Then he focused on Andy Starr, who sat in the passenger seat bleeding from facial cuts.

Starr felt Hosfelt's stare as he applied pressure to his cuts with a handkerchief. He looked up at his young accomplice and nodded. "Thanks. I owe you one," he said.

"Yeah, well, call it a full payback if we get this thing finished as soon as we can and get to New Zealand for some rest. This whole mission's turned into madness . . . sheer madness."

Marc and Carl finished their breakfast and sat quietly, letting their food digest. Carl sipped his coffee while Marc finished what was left of his chocolate malt.

"I don't see how you can drink something like that so early in the morning," Carl said to make small talk. He used his peripheral vision to watch Shirnade and his companion three tables to his right in the tiny dining room.

"It's good for the soul," Marc said wistfully. "Gives you energy."

"Right," Carl said. Then he whispered to Marc. "I don't believe this. That *is* the dude, isn't it?"

"Definitely," Marc replied. "I wonder who his companion is. Tell you what—one of us needs to get up and make it to the rig. Activate the HDTV and get some footage of them when they leave. We can transmit it to Brittin and get him on it. Maybe he can identify her."

Carl nodded. "You finish your malt, and I'll go get the tape rolling. What do we do when they leave, take 'em?"

"No, we follow. I think he can lead us to Dominick," Marc whispered.

"Well, finish your chow, and I'll see you outside," Carl said. He purposely raised his voice so Shirnade and his companion could hear him. He stood from the table, slipped the chair back in place, and walked toward the door without looking at Shirnade or his lady friend.

"See you in a minute," Marc said. He took another sip from his chocolate malt and relaxed in the chair. He glanced around the dining room and caught a glimpse of Shirnade finishing his food. Marc looked for a reflection in the windows or doors that would give him a clear view of the couple without being obvious.

He found it—across the dining room on the north side of the room, facing the street. Marc gazed out the window and concentrated on the reflection of Shirnade and his companion as they completed their breakfast. They were talking in low voices, so Marc couldn't understand what they were saying. He sipped slowly on what little remained of the malt and waited.

Outside, Carl had entered the Leeco rig and activated the concealed high-tech high-definition television cameras and video recorder. He aligned the autotracking devices and put all cameras in motion, switching them automatically as they sent their images to the multichannel two-inch videotape recorder. He also implemented the audio device that would track sounds and send them to a separate master recorder. When he was finished with that, he climbed from the rig and made an inconspicuous stroll around the small gravel parking lot beside the Dairy Delight. Behind the building, two cars were parked close to the rear door. Carl speculated they belonged to the employees. But besides the Leeco rig, there was only one vehicle in the customer parking lot. And that, he hoped, belonged to Shirnade.

Shirnade and his friend stood and walked toward the door.

Marc stood also. He acted as if he didn't see the couple and purposely bumped into Shirnade.

Shirnade stopped abruptly and shot Marc a menacing look.

"Sorry," Marc said. " I didn't know you were behind me. My apologies."

Shirnade stood hard-faced, sized up the man, then broke into an artificial smile. "No problem. We should have watched where we were going."

Marc thought the man's English was impeccable. "Well, got a lot of miles to cover before sundown. You and your lady friend have a good day," Marc said. He gestured toward the door. "After you." Shirnade walked behind Caroline and left the building.

Marc followed. He looked up at the Leeco rig and saw Carl sitting in the driver's seat with the massive diesel engine idling. He stayed four or five steps behind Shirnade, examining him. And he saw it there, the telltale bulge beneath his light jacket, under the left arm. There was no doubt in his mind that Shirnade was armed with some sort of weapon in a shoulder holster. He casually watched every step, sizing up the man.

Shirnade got into the passenger side of the car parked beside the Leeco machine. His female companion got behind the wheel.

Marc climbed aboard the Leeco machine in the passenger seat. He turned to Carl when the car had moved to the edge of the street. "That's our boy. He's carrying in a shoulder holster under his left arm. Also has a mean-looking Rolex on the same arm. Means he's probably right-handed. I have to admire the man for one thing," Marc said, smiling.

"What's that?" Carl asked as he moved onto the street behind the car.

"He has admirable taste in women."

"Can't fault him there," Carl agreed.

"You get it all on tape?" Marc asked.

"Yep, every step of the way."

"Good." Marc lifted the Icom microphone from the cradle and pressed the *transmit* switch. "Barnburner, this is Pathfinder. Over." While he waited for the reply from Brittin Crain, he deactivated the HDTV and rewound the tape through the remote-control pad in the cab.

"Pathfinder, you have traffic?" Crain asked.

"Affirmative," Marc replied. "Get your console ready to receive some wide-band videotape footage. We have a present for you. You'll notice a female in the footage, and the license number of a car. Run everything you can find and try to identify her."

"You find a hot number, or what?" Crain joked.

"Yeah, she's hot, all right. Probably in more ways than one. You'll get the idea when you receive the footage. Say when, and I'll send it over the bird."

"Okay," Crain said. "Let me push a few buttons here, and I'll be ready. Stay on this voice link. I've gotten something you might find of interest also. Okay, that does it. Let the footage roll."

"Rolling," Marc said. He sent the electronic signal to the console in the Leeco trailer, and the video footage was transmitted via satellite.

"Looks like it's coming in good on this end, Pathfinder. Can't wait to see it. Now, we have word that Michigan authorities have located the gray Cadillac believed used by Dominick and friend. There was an old couple in the car. They were abandoned and left unharmed at a rest area just outside Grand Rapids. They were asleep when Dominick and company left them. When they woke up, the hardcases were gone, so they called police. The highway patrol has a team of evidence techs there now. We're expecting a transmission at any moment of fingerprints lifted from the car. We'll run those through the fingerprint-identification computer and see what we can come up with. Maybe, with a little luck, we'll find out who Dominick's running mate is. The old couple verified that there was an encounter with two police cars just after they left Interstate Seventy-five. Where they're going now is anybody's guess. Over."

"Affirmative. Have you made contact with Jill?"

"Roger. She's airborne as we speak. What's up your sleeve anyway?"

"Tell you about it when we get closer. Right now, we're tailing a car that may prove very interesting. You'll see that when you view the footage. Over."

"Roger, I'll yell back at you in a few minutes. I should have something on the satellite-imaging request by the time I get back to you. Barnburner clear."

"Affirmative, Brittin. Pathfinder clear and standing by."

Marc lowered the microphone and looked out at the car. "Stay close, but don't spook 'em," he said.

"No problem," Carl replied. "Wonder who the gal is?"

"I have no idea. She's a looker. It sure makes me wonder how she got involved with someone like Shirnade or Dominick. She could be working for either one of them."

"Don't overlook the obvious. She could be completely clean, with no knowledge of what's going down. That's not very likely though," Carl said.

The car made a left turn down the main street out of Owosso and then sped up. Marc glanced at the Michigan map on the computer screen. "They're headed for Interstate Ninety-six. Got to be. That's the most logical way to the Dunes. Over to Lansing, west to Grand Rapids, northwest toward Muskegon, and backroads to the shores of Lake Michigan. Stay on them."

Carl kept the pace with the car and Omid Shirnade. They moved through moderate traffic, traveling fifty-five to sixty. Fifteen minutes passed, and both vehicles approached the intersection with Interstate 96. The car slowed and chose the westbound lane.

Carl turned the Leeco rig westbound and followed.

The car sped up now and disappeared over a rise a half mile ahead.

"Don't lose 'em," Marc chided.

Carl pressed hard on the accelerator, and the Leeco rig gained more speed. He topped the rise in the highway. When the Highway Warriors had a clear view of the roadway ahead, the car was gone.

Marc slapped the dashboard. "Where the hell did they go? We can't lose them."

"We're not going to lose them," Carl said confidently.

"We run too fast, and we'll get a state trooper on our butts. We can't afford that now."

"Hey, bro, settle down. We have to stop at Grand Rapids to get Jill anyway. We're not going to lose them, trust me."

Marc was very irritated now. "How can you say that?"

"I put a magnetic transponder under the fender well. Bring 'em up on the bird. We can track them to hell and back if they don't change rides."

Chapter Fourteen

□ □ □

Bowman and Warner were relaxed in the comfortable cabin on the shores of Silver Lake when Starr, Dominick, and Hosfelt arrived. Bowman was at the door with the first sound of the Blazer pulling into the short gravel driveway. As soon as the Blazer stopped, Starr was out. He walked toward the front of the cabin, up the steps to the porch, and inside. Dominick and Hosfelt followed.

"Hell of a night, huh, boss?" Bowman asked.

"That's the understatement of the year," Starr said. "Any word from Shirnade or Capenski?"

Bowman walked back across the room and sat down on the sofa. "Yeah, got a call from the broad about an hour ago. They've changed the meet time to three o'clock this afternoon. She said they were running behind due to some kind of problem Shirnade had at the border crossing."

"Yeah, seems to be a lot of that going around . . . problems, that is. Okay, we have to get some bases covered before the meet. First, we've got to get ourselves organized. We took some heavy losses last night and lost some good men. That's something we'll just work around. Are the ATVs all fueled, checked, and ready to go?"

"Yes," Bowman said. Everything is in place. We have all of the radio gear checked out, and we can bring the Blazer or the old truck in at any time."

"Good," Starr said. "Dominick and I are tired, but I think we have to make a test run across the dunes. I want to be absolutely sure everything is functioning. I want to know where Shirnade is every second he's out there on those sand piles. No mistakes. God knows we've already made enough of 'em. We cannot, under any circumstances, afford any more. The heat is on, and it's looking to scorch our asses. Let's get things right this time."

Warner stood from the kitchen table and stopped beside Starr. "When do you want to make the runs?"

"How soon can you have the equipment loaded and ready?"

Warner looked confident. "Ten minutes, maybe less. Is everybody going?"

"Yes, this needs to be a dry run for the real thing. We need to evaluate our positions and make more timing runs. We can't mess it up. Get the gear, and let's take a ride."

"Okay," Warner said. "You coming?" he asked Bowman.

"Right behind you," Bowman replied.

"I'll give them a hand," Hosfelt said.

All three men left the cabin and climbed into Hosfelt's Blazer. Then they left the driveway and disappeared on the winding road beside Silver Lake.

Dominick sat on the sofa and lit his first cigar since he had left the cabin a day before. He relaxed, propped his feet on the already-scuffed coffee table, and leaned back against the soft cushion. He stared at Andy Starr and made no effort to hide his contempt. "I hope you know what you're doing. This whole thing has come unraveled."

"Yes, it has come unraveled. Think about it for a moment. Your informants gave us the inside scoop on the PNDs. They're the ones who made the mistake. Either somebody made them, or they turned on us. The feds know who you are, and they know what has happened. What they don't know is our intentions for the stolen devices. We can't let them find out, either. We have to make the deal, get the money, and get out of this country as quickly as possible."

"You make it sound so easy," Dominick said, and he took a deep draw off the cigar.

"It's as simple as we make it. The important thing is that we take care of Shirnade. He must not get his hands on the PNDs or the plutonium until we have confirmation of the money. The second thing is that we manage, somehow, to avoid the heat until we complete the deal. It couldn't be much simpler. If we can accomplish those two things, I'll get all of us out of the country. Count on it."

"I *am* counting on it," Dominick said. "Let's go to the park entrance and get on with the trial run. I want to see what these four-by-fours are made of."

Dominick and Starr left the cabin and got into a four-wheel-drive pickup truck parked outside. They drove along the scenic winding roadway beside Silver Lake until they reached an intersection. There, they turned left and drove the short distance to the entrance of the Dunes State Park. They paid the entrance fee to the park attendant and drove out the sandy road toward the towering mounds of sand that had been swept inland by time and the currents of Lake Michigan.

Starr moved the pickup into four-wheel drive and proceeded up a sandy path that was the road. When the vehicle started upward on the winding trail toward the top of the high mounds, he dropped the selector into four-wheel low and reduced his speed. The special wide off-road tires made travel easy.

Starr reached the top of the first massive dune and stopped. To the west, the surface of Lake Michigan glittered blue as far as the eye could see. Across the slightly choppy water, whitecaps painted disappearing light streaks across the otherwise blue water. Down near the shore, a mile away at the bottom of the dunes, perpetual waves crashed lazily into the sandy beach, sweeping new sand ashore with every motion. From there the sand, dried by the brilliant rays of an unrestricted sun, would fly inland to form more monumental dunes. Over time, the shifting sands had conquered a large portion of the inland Silver Lake. Estimates by the scientific community speculated that Silver Lake would become just another dune sometime within the next hundred years. But right now, Andy Starr wasn't worried about that.

He stopped there for several minutes and surveyed the rolling mounds of sand. He glanced back across Lake Michigan, noticed a freighter moving in a shipping channel somewhere near the horizon, and hoped the *Polly P* was resting comfortably in her grave at the bottom of the massive body of water.

"Breathtaking, isn't it?" Dominick said.

Starr hesitated and didn't answer for a long moment. He looked south and saw Warner, Hosfelt, and Bowman trailing toward him on ATVs from the crest of another dune a mile away. Orange triangular flags flew eight feet above their machines, dancing in the wind at the end of a long white fiberglass shaft required of all vehicles operating on the dunes. "Not as breathtaking as it will be if it goes up in a mushroom cloud. But I guess that depends on Shirnade and the feds, huh?"

Caroline saw the sign for the approaching exit and turned onto the exit ramp ten miles outside Grand Rapids. When she reached the end of the ramp, she saw the giant sign for the truck-stop parking lot. She went a quarter of a mile, and turned left into the truck-stop lot. She found a parking space in front of the truck-stop restaurant. Then she glanced down at her watch. "We're five minutes early. Shall we go inside and take a table?"

"Yes," Omid said. "This person with whom we meet is a trustworthy one, yes?"

"He's clean and dependable. He doesn't care what he hauls or who he hauls it for as long as he's paid in cash. That, of course, we will do. He will deliver wherever we designate and arrive at precisely the appointed time. I have used him before when we were shipping computer technology behind the iron curtain. He is efficient. Shall we go inside?"

Omid opened his door, stood on the pavement, and stretched his legs. He looked over the top of the car at Caroline. "It feels good to stand. Riding makes me stiffen. It must come with increasing age."

"I think you have some time before you must be concerned about that, Omid," she said. "A cup of coffee before our appointment?"

They entered the restaurant, saw the hostess, and followed her to a table. They got comfortable in their seats and sipped on glasses of ice water. Caroline watched the restaurant entrance for the familiar face of her transportation connection.

Then she saw him. She glanced at her watch out of habit and realized he was precisely on time, to the minute. She nodded her head when the man looked her way. He walked slowly to the table.

Caroline stood when the man stopped beside the table and shook his hand. "Richard, how are you? It has been a while."

Richard accepted her hand and looked at Omid inquisitively. "I'm fine, Caroline. It's good to see you again."

Caroline smiled. "Richard, I would like you to meet my friend Omid Shirnade. We occasionally transact some business together."

Omid stood. "Richard, it's a pleasure to meet you.

Caroline speaks well of your skills." Richard and Omid shook hands.

"I'm sorry, Omid, this is Richard Brandon," Caroline said.

"No apology necessary, Caroline. Shall we all be seated?"

Everyone sat at the table and exchanged pleasantries while the waitress took their orders. Caroline and Omid ordered coffee, and Richard decided to have a full meal.

Caroline looked into Richard's eyes. "Do you have the ATVs, Richard?" She asked.

"You ordered them and paid me for them, didn't you? Of course I have them. They're in the back of the rig. Two big bright red Honda four-bys. They have extra-capacity fuel tanks, and the radio antennas were mounted just where you said they should be to attach to the two-way walkie-talkies. I have those too. Motorola P-two-hundreds and those little speaker-and-microphone combinations."

"Excellent," said Caroline. "Now, I will give you delivery instructions before we leave here. When you make the delivery, keep a radio with you. Should a change in our loading situation occur, I want to be able to contact you."

"Ain't no problem. You've hired me and my rig for the next thirty days if you want us," Brandon said.

"I only need you for a week, maybe less," Caroline said.

"Lady, another customer or two like you, and I'd just work two or three weeks a year. You name the game, and I'll play it. Me and *Lady Luck* are all yours," Brandon said, smiling.

"'Lady Luck'?" Shirnade asked. "I thought Caroline said you worked alone."

Brandon laughed. "Hell, boy, come to the party. *Lady Luck* is my rig. The eighteen-wheeler."

"Oh," Shirnade said. "Please accept my apology for my ignorance."

"No harm done," Brandon said. "Now just what is it you want me to do, Miss Caroline?"

"I want you to go to Silver Lake with the ATVs. When you get there, go to a cabin on the second road to your right after you turn off onto the road that leads straight to the base of the dunes. The cabin will have red shutters and a black roof. The front is painted white. There will be a mailbox out front with a—what is it called—country-craft design on it. There is no number, so you must be aware of my description. Are you with me so far?"

"Yes," Brandon said. He scribbled notes in a small notebook as Caroline spoke.

"Now," Caroline continued. "Unload the ATVs there. You have a cabin rented there also. It is a half mile away. Go to the rental agency near the restaurant at Silver Lake. They will have your name and give you instructions for your cabin. Omid and I will take care of our business and call you on the radio. When you get the call, come to the Silver Lake State Park exit. We will meet you there. We will have several crates to be transported. Once you have these crates, you must go directly to the destination we give you, without stopping. This material is very fragile, and it must not have an opportunity to end up in improper hands."

"In other words, this stuff is as hot as a three-dollar pistol, right?" Brandon asked.

"That's irrelevant. Just say many people would like to have what is in those cartons."

"Okay, I'll leave it at that. I don't think I care to know," Brandon said. He sipped from his glass of water. "What then?"

"Reach the destination, and someone will meet us to take care of the cargo."

"Sounds simple," Brandon said. Then his voice changed. "What's the catch?"

"The catch is, many people would kill you for what will be in that truck. No one except you, me, and Omid must know when it's in there. All our lives could depend on it."

"Wait a minute. You said, 'Someone will meet us'? Who is 'us'?" Brandon asked.

Caroline's face split with a radiant smile. "You and me. I'm riding with you, once the cargo is loaded."

"How nice," Brandon said. "You and me, *swampers.*"

"What is a 'swamper'?" Omid asked.

"Another driver," Brandon said. "You know, a person that swaps in the hot seat dodging old Smokey. A *swamper.*"

"I suppose I should let it go, hey?" Shirnade said, admitting his confusion.

"Yes," Caroline said. She looked back at Brandon. "Do you have any questions on anything, Richard? If so, now is the time to ask them."

"Well, just one, Miss Caroline. This stuff I'm hauling ain't gonna blow up, is it?"

Caroline's face tightened, and her muscles tensed. "I certainly hope not, Richard. I *really* do."

"The beacon's been stopped for several minutes," Marc said. "According to the map, they're at the next exit, just off the connecting highway."

"Must be a pee break," Carl replied.

"That, or a switch," Marc said.

"Could be. Want to go take a look?"

"I think it would be in our best interest. But even if they change vehicles, I don't think there's much doubt about where they're going. My question is whether or not the PNDs are at those sand dunes or somewhere nearby. Could be they're going there to make other arrangements."

"That gal sure did push her Chevy. I don't believe how far she got ahead of us. If they don't do the deal at the Dunes, they're going to have to move fast. Dominick is a hot number. With his face in every major newspaper in the country and on all the television networks, he's going to find it tough to hide for too long. Somebody's going to recognize him and make a call. I'd rather we find him before that happens."

"Something else bothers me," said Marc. "We're relying heavily on the information Brittin secured from the company. If we're running on the assumption that the information is accurate and Shirnade *is* involved, and it turns out we're wrong . . . hell, man, I don't even want to think about the consequences."

"It's all we've got right now," Carl said. "Besides, the coincidence is just too great. Think about it—Shirnade turns up in a small quiet Michigan town . . . Owosso. He could have been in Detroit, Lansing, Grand Rapids—anywhere but Owosso. Now what's outside of Owosso? The testing and research facility for personal nuclear weapons, right? Only in a small town could we stumble into Shirnade. Now the rascal is moving in a beeline for the most logical place to make a deal on something as hot as stolen military weapons. The Dunes. Couple that with the information that clown at the trucking terminal gave us a night or two ago, and the conclusion is only logical. This hot ticket from the Middle East has to be in on the deal. Dominick is the thief, and Shirnade's the fence. Simple as that."

"Maybe too simple," Marc said. "You're discounting Shirnade's female companion. Where does she fit in? Dominick and his band of hoodlums aren't doing this because they're bored. His track record speaks for itself. He's a common thief with a champagne appetite."

"He's also a killer," Carl said. "He's got to have connections somewhere high up the totem pole, or he couldn't have unearthed Compton as the fed's mole. Another few days, and Compton's information would have toppled Dominick's scheme. That's why the guy's dead. He got too close, and Dominick got information from somewhere that burned him. Maybe if we'd been a few hours earlier, the guy would still be alive, and this madness never would have happened."

"Too many people have died because of Tommy Dominick. The security troops, all those people at the rest area, those cops . . . we've got to find him and take him and his thugs down. I just hope we aren't barking up the wrong tree with Shirnade."

"Here's the exit," Carl said. He slowed the rig in the right lane and made the exit. "Got a solid mark on the transponder?"

"End of ramp, right, then immediate left," Marc replied as he inspected the computerized map with a blinking red cursor on the computer screen.

Carl looked to the end of the ramp and in the general direction of the transponder's signal. "The truck stop. I'll be damned."

"Let's take a look," Marc said.

Carl rolled to the end of the exit ramp, turned right, and then drove to the truck stop. He turned the Leeco rig into the lot and immediately saw the blue Chevy that had been driven by Shirnade's companion. "There it is, in front of the restaurant."

"Yeah," Marc said. "But are Shirnade and his lady friend inside?"

"There's one way to find out. Soon as I park this thing, we can go inside and take a look," Carl said.

"Park where I can watch the car. You go inside," Marc said. "Shirnade got too good a look at me back at the Dairy Delight. I don't want to spook him if he's in there. I don't think he'll remember you."

"Deal," Carl replied.

"I'll get on the horn and see if anything new has developed while you're inside."

Carl parked the rig seventy-five yards from the Chevy and headed inside.

Marc focused on the car. He activated the HDTV system again and zoomed the front camera in on the car. Then he lifted the Icom microphone from its cradle and called Brittin Crain. "Barnburner, this is Pathfinder. How copy? Over."

Seconds passed, then Crain answered from the control room in downtown Washington. "Pathfinder, you have traffic?"

"Affirmative. How'd you like the morning movie, old buddy?"

"Real fine. Got the computers and a team of ID folks working on the girl. The company confirms your man is Shirnade. Data imaging of his composite is a perfect match. What's the story on him, anyway? You got his number?"

"Yeah," Marc said into the microphone. "We're stopped at a truck stop west of Grand Rapids. The car is here, and Carl's inside making a visual check. Should know something in a minute. We're hoping this stop wasn't a planned switch for transportation. Over."

"Affirmative," Crain said. "Got those satellite images you requested of that place you call the Dunes. It's a negative. The military people tell me that wouldn't be unusual if there has been no breach in the integrity of the original packaging of the plutonium. Also, the PNDs shouldn't be hot until they're armed. I do have complete topo maps of the area that I can fax to you if you still want them. Over."

"Roger," Marc said. "The system is on-line. Go ahead whenever you're ready. Any word from Jill?"

"Talked to Placeway at the Pentagon just a few minutes ago. The Lear should be on final approach as we speak. What's up your sleeve, anyway?"

"Just thought I'd like to have some female company when I stroll Michigan's massive sand dunes. That should help my cover. What's the word on the chemical spill at the rest area?"

"Cleanup crews working on it hard and heavy. FEMA has three crisis-management teams there. Death toll is gonna be a bitch on that one. The Boss is at Camp David, and he's not a happy camper with all the negative press. They think the shifting wind is taking the stuff into the upper atmosphere. Speculation has it that it should dissipate harmlessly if it stays aloft. The upside to that is if the thing had ruptured at morning or afternoon drivetime, the death toll would have probably been ten times what it is. Guess we have to look for something positive in all this, huh?"

"Roger," Marc said. "Carl's coming out. I'll get back with you when I can. Roger?"

"Roger, Marc. Barnburner standing by."

Carl returned to the rig and climbed aboard. He settled in the driver's seat. "They're in there, all right. Got a guy with 'em that looks like he's a trucker. Could be a mule for their deal."

"Good," Marc said. "Let's off-load one of the Jeeps. The Learjet should be down in Grand Rapids by now. You stay with the rig and follow Shirnade. I'll take the Jeep and get Jill. Then I'm going on to the Dunes and snoop around. Maybe, if Dominick is there, I can sniff him out. I'll stay on the ComSat-D link and meet you when you get there. If anything changes, yell."

"We'd better move fast," Carl said as he stared at the blue Chevy in front of the restaurant. "Take a look. Shirnade and his friend are moving."

Marc glanced toward the car and the truck-stop building. "Okay, bro, let's get it done."

Chapter Fifteen

□ □ □

Richard Brandon, unaware of Marc Lee behind him in the Jeep Cherokee, followed the directions Caroline Capenski had given him. He drove the rig slowly over the narrow roadway that wove along the shore of Silver Lake at the base of the giant mountains of shifting sand that composed the Dunes. Small wooden boat docks dotted the shoreline, built by cabin owners and boat-leasing operators and jutting into the cold, crystal waters of the mirror-like lake. In front of him, the golden sand extended from the edge of the water's surface and seemed to touch the clouds in rolling pinnacles that shifted and changed in the ever-present winds. Atop the dunes, tiny figures, people at play, dotted the horizon.

Brandon spotted the cabin with red shutters and saw the mailbox, decorated just as Caroline had said. He moved the rig slightly past it, calculated his angles, and backed the huge eighteen-wheeler into the narrow gravel driveway. When he had the front end of the cab barely off the roadway, he kicked the machine into neutral, set the brake, and climbed out to check the unloading clearances at the back. When he got there, he saw he had just enough room to open the door, extend the small loading ramp, and move the Honda ATV four-by-fours out of the trailer.

He went back to the cab, shut the diesel engine off, and went to unload.

Marc drove the highly customized black Jeep Cherokee slowly past the red-shuttered cabin. Carl had identified Brandon's rig back at the truck stop and radioed the information ahead to Marc, who picked the rig up when it arrived at the Dunes. Jill Lanier, friend, sometime lover, and companion in the war against evil, sat in the passenger seat. Her honey-blond hair was tied neatly in a ponytail with the knot of a red bandanna she wore stylishly around her head. She gazed out the windows through her sunglasses, awed by the scenic beauty of Silver Lake and the Dunes. In her best performance, she emulated a carefree tourist.

Jill looked away after the Jeep rolled past the cabin. She looked to her left at Marc Lee, and beyond him to the glittering surface of Silver Lake. "Looks like he's unloading some ATVs. That sounds rather convenient, doesn't it."

"Like I told you on the way here, there are many things that sound very convenient about this operation," Marc said. He reached the end of the narrow road along the shore and circled a giant oak tree that with time would fall victim to the shifting sands of the Dunes. He made the tight circular turn and headed back in the direction from which he had come. Beside the oak tree, at the end of the road, the apex of a cabin roof barely protruded through the surface of the sand. The cabin, like others that would follow, had been lost to the sea of shifting silicon particles.

Marc stopped the Jeep beside a NO-PARKING sign and shut off the engine. First, he radioed the location of the house back to Carl, then he reached into the backseat and retrieved a pair of rubber-armored 10 x 50 binoculars. He lifted the small silenced Uzi from beside the seat, slipped it over his shoulder, and managed to slip a black field jacket on over it. "Grab your jacket, and let's take a stroll in the sand."

Jill gazed at him conspicuously. "With boots on?"

"Barefoot. Take your boots off, and let's go to the top." Marc leaned over and removed his boots, then his socks. He rolled the legs of his jeans up around his knees. He wiggled his toes and smiled. "Ah, I can already feel the soothing sand between my toes."

Jill looked out the window at the mountain of sand beside the Jeep. "That looks like a tough climb in unsettled sand," she said.

"Just pretend you're walking in warm snow," Marc said. He looked at Jill's azure-blue eyes. They made him smile and feel warm inside. And that was a feeling he didn't seem to have often enough anymore—not since the beginning of the nightmare that he, Carl, and Jill had come to think of as a never-ending war. For a moment, he found himself lost in her eyes. But then reality came back to him. "It's about the same. You'll be up to your knees before you know it. The top of the dune looks like a good vantage point to scope this place out. We'll look just like another happy tourist couple away from the grind for a little R and R."

"Speaking of which, when are you and I going to get away from this madness and take a little private R and R?"

Marc's voice mellowed. "Someday. I promise. Let's go."

Marc secured the Jeep, and they left it and walked ten feet to the edge of the sand. "Here we go," Marc said. He led the way in the warm loose sand and started toward the top of the huge dune.

Jill looked behind her. "Wow, that's amazing."

"What?" Marc asked.

"You can't even see where we walked. It's like no one was ever there. Our trail is gone almost as soon as we take another step."

"Guess now we understand the cliché about the shifting sands of time, huh?" Marc replied. "It covers and devours everything equally. Just like a nuclear explosion."

They walked and climbed, the sand moving and shifting beneath their feet. Fifteen minutes passed and Marc stopped for a break. He looked back at Jill, who had broken into a glistening sweat. "How are you feeling?"

"Boy, this is like work," she said breathlessly. She looked back toward Silver Lake. People walking on the shore looked like tiny dots. Motorized boats looked more like paper clips on a mirror than boats in water. "I feel like I have to yell so you can hear me. This wind is incredible. And when the flying sand hits you, it stings like needles."

"Not much farther to go, and we'll be at the top of the first one," Marc said.

"The first one?" Jill quizzed.

"Yeah, they roll on for miles. We'll stop on top and have a look around. Ready?"

Ten more minutes passed, and Marc could see the top of the first high dune. He turned to Jill again. "Not far now," he said.

"Look out!" Jill screamed. She leapt forward and tackled Marc around the waist. They hit the sand and rolled downhill only an instant before the first ATV landed in the very spot where they had stood.

Then the top of the dune came alive with more ATVs. Four in all. They flew from the crest of the dune and landed twenty or thirty feet from the top down the side where Marc and Jill had walked. Their impact sent a shower of sand into the air.

Marc and Jill covered their heads and eyes against the pelting sand. Then, in seconds, the ATVs were gone as quickly and silently as they had come.

"Damn," Marc said. "I owe you one. I didn't hear those things."

"Neither did I," Jill said. "If I hadn't been looking in that direction, I wouldn't have known they were there."

"Whoever they were, they sure were reckless. Let's make the best of it. This is as good a place as any to take a look around."

They sat upright and settled into the sand. Marc retrieved the binoculars, just before Carl's voice crackled across the speaker of the Icom U-16 clipped to his belt. "Hey, bro, our boy and his lady are moving toward the cabin where the truck went. They're in the blue Chevy. Four hardcase types in two four-bys coming in close behind them. They met a little way back out the road. I think the team is taking shape. I'm going to lie back and watch the entrance to the road."

"Roger," Marc said as he lifted the Icom and pressed the rubber-covered *talk* switch on the side. "Better go ahead and unload the other Jeep so we can get the ATVs out in a hurry. I think it's almost party time."

"Where the hell did those people come from?" Andy Starr screamed into the helmet-mounted microphone as he negotiated the four-by-four all-terrain vehicle toward the next dune. "I thought we had their asses. That's all we need. Move to the bottom, and let's park these things until it's time for the meet. We've done enough until then."

Dominick's voice crackled through the headset. "I'm rolling your way, guys. Be there in a minute. This old truck is tough on this sand pile, but it's not as fast as those four-bys."

"Ten-four," Starr said. "We're at the bottom of the second dune south of the trail leading into the park. We'll wait."

Little more than a minute passed, and the nose of Dominick's modified dune-buggy pickup truck appeared at the top of the dune. Then the big truck cleared the crest and headed down the side of the dune like an ant descending an anthill. The mufflerless truck stopped at the bottom of the dune and slid in the sand. Its engine died to a gurgling rumble. Dominick shut it off and climbed out. "Hell, boys, this could be fun if we weren't in such a hurry. Maybe we'll have to make a trip to Baja when this thing is done."

"Right," Starr said. "Let's be done with it before we start spending the money. You still got the sample in the back of the truck."

"Still there," Dominick replied.

Starr checked his watch. "Okay, guys, mount up. Two of you, Warner and Bowman, take your bikes to the top and stage around that area. Hosfelt, come with us. We'll call you on the two-way when we get the call from Shirnade. When we come to the top for the meet, Rick will be in the truck. Tommy and I will be on four-bys. I'm carrying the detonator, and Rick will have the sample." He paused and looked at Hosfelt. "Rick, if this thing mushrooms and goes nuts up there, touch off that round and get the hell away from here. You can hit a target from one dune to the other with your eyes closed. Maybe most of you guys can escape. I don't know. Warner, you and Bowman stay out of sight unless things deteriorate and we yell for you. I don't want this clown spooked. More than anything else, I don't want him to leave this sandbox alive if the deal goes sour. Any questions?"

No one answered.

Starr motioned toward the truck with his right arm. "Okay, let's move out and wait for the turkey's call."

Richard Brandon had already left the red-shuttered cabin when Shirnade and Caroline arrived. Caroline exited the car first and led the way to the front porch. She unlocked the door with the key she had picked up from the rental agency and went inside, followed by Shirnade.

"Would you like to tour the accommodations?" she asked Shirnade.

"It isn't necessary, really. We won't be here that long." He checked the time on his Rolex. "Perhaps we should make the call, hey?"

Caroline verified the time by her own watch. "Well, we *are* a couple minutes early, but I see no harm in that." She walked to the telephone on a tattered end table at the end of the sofa. She picked up the receiver and dialed the number she had memorized days before. The line rang.

"Yes?" the answering voice inquired. It was Rick Hosfelt.

"I have business with Mr. Dominick," Caroline said.

"Yeah, just a minute," said Hosfelt.

Caroline sat relaxed on the edge of the sofa while Shirnade paced around the small living room.

"Yes," Dominick said.

"I have something you want. Do you have what I want?" Caroline asked pleasantly when she recognized Dominick's voice.

"Yes, just as we agreed," Dominick replied nervously.

"Where might I see it?"

"Top dune. The highest one, south of the entrance to the state park. Fifteen minutes. Two of us. One red and one orange triangle on the safety poles. Both four-by-fours. A red helmet and a black one. Any questions?"

"There will be two of us also. We will be on two Honda four-by-fours, both red. Our safety markers are orange, and our shafts are black. No additional guests, please. Agreed?"

"Agreed," Dominick said.

"I will see you in exactly fifteen minutes from now. Good day."

Caroline hung up and smiled at Shirnade. "It's a go. Let's move fast."

"They're rolling," Carl said into the microphone. "They're getting on the Hondas now. Step on it."

"Be there in a couple of minutes," Marc replied. "You got the four-bys out?"

"Roger. They'll be warm by the time you get here."

"Let's go babe," Marc said. "The game is on."

"How are we going to get down from this sand dune?" Jill asked, puzzled.

"Like this," Marc said. He stood and started running. He hit the edge of the dune toward the Jeep Cherokee and ran hard. He jumped, taking ten feet at a shot, and landed in the sand, sank to his knees, and jumped again. When he looked behind him, Jill was airborne also.

In less than two minutes, they were at the bottom, and Marc had the Jeep's doors opened. They were both laughing and almost out of breath. "Hop in. We've got to move fast," Marc said.

"Killjoy," Jill replied.

Marc fired the engine and shifted the Jeep into gear. He spun hard on the loose sand, but the tires finally caught, and the Jeep sped forward. "Okay, when we reach Carl, I want you to take this Cherokee and follow us. You'll be perfectly safe inside here. Gunfire can't penetrate it. I'll take one four-by, and Carl will take the other. When we hit them, if this is the meet, lay back until I give you the word over the radio. Your optic helmet will control the weapons systems, and you'll have both hands free to drive. Be careful up there. You saw how those dunes roll and drop off into nothing."

"The Jeep will protect me from gunfire. What happens if they decide to detonate those nuclear devices?"

"Don't worry about it," Marc said. "You'll never know it."

"Why isn't that comforting?" Jill replied.

Marc sped past the red-shuttered cabin. Shirnade and his friend were gone. He continued to the end of the road and slid to a stop beside the Leeco rig.

Carl was waiting, helmet on, the customized all-terrain vehicles idling.

Marc rolled from the Cherokee. "It's all yours," he said to Jill.

"Be careful, Marc. I love you," she replied as he slipped toward the driver's seat.

"I love you too. Follow us and watch the backsides. Later," he said, and he ran from the Jeep to the ATV. He put on his optic helmet, adjusted it, and kicked the machine into gear. "Okay, boys and girls, it's showtime."

Tommy Dominick and Andy Starr were waiting atop the highest dune south of the state park entrance when they saw the orange triangles waving at the end of the poles on Caroline Capenski's and Omid Shirnade's off-road ATVs. The ATVs were coming at high speed toward the peak.

"Here they come, Dominick. It's time to do your stuff," Starr said. "Remember, if it goes astray, get the hell out of Dodge and let me and my men take care of the rest."

"Got it," Dominick said.

The ATVs rolled to a stop in front of Starr and Dominick. Caroline flipped the Plexiglas visor up on her helmet and looked at Starr and Dominick. "You have what we want, I trust?"

"Yes," Dominick said coldly. "And you have what we want?"

"I do. There has, however, been a slight change of plans along that line."

"And what might that be?" Dominick asked. He tried

to remain cool, but the mention of change sent butterflies churning through his stomach.

"We decided it's best not to do the transfer. Omid has brought cash instead. I hope you will find that acceptable," Caroline said.

Dominick hesitated, his heart racing. "Why the change? Why did you not confer with me first?"

"Last minute necessities," Caroline said. "With the exposure you have given this transaction and the potential problems your problems could cause, we decided a transfer of money into your name or anyone who could be traced to you would not be in the best interest of our benefactors. If you would prefer that we cancel the transaction . . . well, that can still happen."

"You have five million dollars in cash with you?" Dominick asked. He was excited now.

"That is correct. Do you have the sample ready for our examination?" Caroline asked. She squinted her eyes against the force of sand blowing in the wind.

"Yes, we have it. You show us the money, and we will show the sample device," Dominick said. He kept his voice cool and firm.

"We have a driver near the bottom of the dunes. I can call him, if necessary, to bring the money. Where is the device?"

"Right behind you," Dominick said. He pointed to the pickup truck driven by Rick Hosfelt. "Call your driver. When he is within view, I'll call my man in with the device."

"Very well," Caroline said. She lifted the microphone attached to the Motorola P-200 transceiver and made the call. "Bring it to me, please."

Dominick lifted his handheld and called to Hosfelt. "Rick, bring it here when you see another vehicle crest the dune."

Seconds passed like hours, and then the two four-wheel-drive vehicles were side by side, moving toward the high dune and the meeting. Both vehicles stopped, and the drivers got out. Rick Hosfelt walked to the back of the truck and shouldered a device slightly larger than a LAW-class rocket launcher. He walked beside Starr and Dominick, and stopped.

The driver of the other four-wheel-drive truck walked forward also. He carried a large leather case, smaller than a medium suitcase but larger than an attaché case. He stopped beside Caroline and Shirnade.

"You see mine. May I see yours?" Dominick said.

Caroline nodded to the driver, and he opened the case. Inside were neat rows of stacked United States hundred-dollar bills. "Five million American dollars. You may count it if you feel the need to." Caroline nodded again, and the man shut the case, then snapped the latches closed.

"I think not. If it's short, we know where to find both of you," Dominick said confidently.

"Where are the remaining units and the plutonium?" Caroline asked.

"Safely nestled in the shifting sand. We will take you to them as soon as you give us the money. We were prepared to confirm the transfer of funds before delivery, but you've made this much simpler," Dominick said.

Caroline nodded again, and the man passed the leather case to Dominick. Dominick accepted and immediately handed it to Hosfelt.

"Follow us," said Dominick. "We will take you to the remaining devices."

"As you wish. We will bring the truck to haul them. Is that a problem?" Caroline asked.

"Not with me," Dominick said. He fired the starter on his ATV, and Starr did the same. Hosfelt took the leather case and returned to the pickup truck. "This way," Dominick said.

All of the ATVs and the two pickup trucks rolled across the dunes like vacationers enjoying the challenging crooks, curves, and jumps of the massive sand mounds. They rode across the mighty sand until they were out of the state park and on sand leased to a tour company. Andy Starr led the way while all of the others followed single file.

The ride took ten minutes, but finally after a sandy roller-coaster run, Starr stopped at a spot he had marked mentally by triangulation using the sun-scorched remnants of dead trees for markers. The spot was just under the crest of the dune on the south side, thirty-five feet from the top. He looked up at Caroline and Shirnade. "Have your man dig here, and he will find the devices and the plutonium."

"How deep?" Caroline asked.

"Not very," Starr replied.

Caroline nodded to the pickup driver again, and he moved to the spot designated by Starr. He dug feverishly for a couple of minutes, then uncovered the first crate. He brought it to Caroline and put it down.

Omid produced a heavy-bladed knife and pried the wooden top from the crate. Inside lay a gleaming new personal nuclear device. "Nice," he murmured.

"There are more," the driver said.

"Good. Very good." Omid produced a small pistol before anyone could move. "Now, I will take our money back and leave your wretched bones for the vultures."

Starr laughed. "I don't think so, sand flea," he said. In his hands was a small transmitter. "The crates are all booby-trapped. You can't kill me fast enough to keep me from pressing this button. When I do, these sandpiles will be nothing but craters. And all of us, my untrustworthy friend, will be ashes burning in hell."

Chapter Sixteen

□ □ □

"Now!" Marc said into the voice-actuated headset.

Carl unleashed a single round from the infrared-sighted Stinger miniguns on the front of his ATV. The round struck Starr's arm a full half second before the sound of the shot rolled across the dunes.

Marc and Carl were in motion at the same time. They split, going in different directions. Their customized ATVs moved like lightning across the steep dunes. And while they moved, streaks of hellfire belched from the fender-mounted machined guns.

Starr jerked his arm away in pain, and the transmitter fell to the sand, then slid aimlessly down the steep side of the dune.

Omid reacted, turning hard and firing his automatic pistol before he even saw the target. When he realized hell had come to the dunes, he jumped aboard his ATV and fired the engine. He slid sideways, fishtailing, then sped across the side of the high sandpile.

Caroline was behind him. Lead from Marc's machine guns sprayed sand all around her as she struggled to get in her ATV. She made it and streaked across the dunes behind Omid.

Dominick panicked. He looked first at Starr, then at

the streaks of hellfire blazing from the ATVs charging at him. He jumped into his ATV, opened the throttle, and headed across the mound of sand in a direction diagonally away from Omid and Caroline.

Rick Hosfelt dove for the passenger door on the pickup. He made it, got it open, slid behind the steering wheel, and fired the rumbling engine. He shifted into gear, and the pickup slipped and slid, then tore across the top of the dune.

Marc closed hard on the man who had driven the pickup for Caroline. The man retrieved an automatic pistol from beneath his shirt and fired wildly toward the approaching ATVs. Marc aligned the sights for the Stinger miniguns on the guy's chest and unsheathed a long burst of death. The sizzlers caught the guy midway in his chest and ripped through him like a swarm of angry hornets. Where his chest had been, an open cavity of blood flooded his clothing. He lurched backward, hit the sand tumbling, and toppled down the steep slope toward a long ravine.

Marc turned his attention toward Shirnade. He opened the throttle on the ATV and spun out in pursuit. When he topped the first dune south of him, he saw the flag sailing in the wind atop Shirnade's ATV. He hit the custom machine for all he could get and closed the gap.

Meanwhile, Carl went after Dominick and Starr, who had regrouped and fled along the western bottom of the mighty sandpiles. They were on the shore of Lake Michigan now, running full throttle. A mist of sand and water flew in their wake as they fled northward.

Carl hit the bottom of the dunes and headed up the lake's shoreline. He opened the custom machine full throttle and moved in closer.

Suddenly, Dominick cut to the right and started back up the dunes. Then he stopped abruptly and jumped from the machine. He crouched low behind the seat, came out with an AK-47, and opened fire, 7.62 X 39mm death pellets slamming into the wet sand around Carl. Twice he even heard the whistle as bullets narrowly missed his head.

Carl spun right, leveled the optic sight on the ATV, and unleashed a minirocket from the side-mounted pod. A streak of white smoke trailed all the way to the ATV and Tommy Dominick. The streak stopped at the perimeter of a glowing red ball of fire that shook the earth along the shoreline. Dominick was incinerated and on his way to hell before he had time to realize that he was dead.

Carl cut back to the left and continued his pursuit of Andy Starr, who was now a full quarter mile down the shoreline. The ATV reared into the air, its front wheels leaving the ground, then settled back as Carl pushed the machine to its design specifications and beyond.

Caroline Capenski had been scared before, but not like this. She had, even with her vast training, never seen machines like the ones that were attacking them now. Never had she seen weapons like those mounted on an ATV. And never had anyone fired on her with weapons that demanded such respect. Who were these people who had materialized from nowhere. At the moment, she wasn't going to stop and ask them.

Caroline opened the throttle, and the ATV went airborne over the edge of a crest. She landed fifty feet down the side and hit the brakes as she struggled to hold on. She reached the bottom of the ravine and sped as fast as she could up the other side. Then she cut hard to the left and moved along the rim of the dune toward the park entrance where she knew she could get to Richard Brandon and the eighteen-wheeler. He, and probably only he, held her ticket away from the hellfire that sought to devour her. She didn't know that he was already gone at the first sounds of gunfire.

She cut right, down another dune, bottomed out, and went up the other side. She didn't see the men with the strange-looking off-road machines and could no longer hear the gunfire. That meant either the frenzy had calmed or everyone was dead. She didn't know which. Right now, she didn't care.

Her ATV climbed hard up the loose sand and hit the crest on the fly. Caroline throttled out hard and hit a small rise before going over the edge again, airborne. When the ATV headed down a long descent, she opened the machine up, giving it all the gas she could. She hit the bottom once more and headed up the other side. When she crested that dune and hit the sand, she slammed on the brakes, and the ATV careened wildly. She stopped ten feet from the front of a gleaming black Jeep Cherokee.

Caroline looked over the vehicle for a second. She saw Jill Lanier behind the wheel and screamed at her. "Get that thing out of my way, bitch!"

Jill didn't move.

Caroline reached beneath her windbreaker and came out with a small submachine gun. She held the little weapon at arm's length and cut loose a burst of 9mm death pellets.

The stream hit the Jeep, spent their energy harmlessly, and dissipated above the sandy dunes.

Jill pressed the transmit switch for the PA system mounted under the Jeep's hood, the speaker behind the grille. Her voice was cold and authoritative. "Quit while you can, or the next shot is mine. And I warn you, I don't miss."

Marc had Omid Shirnade in his sights. He started to fire instant death toward the man but changed his mind. He wanted him alive if possible.

Omid glanced over his shoulder and saw the awesome

ATV closing on him. He cut hard right and flew over the lip of the dune. He trailed hard down the side of the steep slope and hit the bottom full throttle.

Marc was directly behind him. He ran all out now, taxing the machine, and remembered what the designer had told him long ago: "Don't let this thing get away from you." He let it roll full bore anyway. He was almost beside Shirnade now. Then he aligned the optical sight and tapped out a burst of full-auto fire from the miniguns. The sizzlers slammed into the rear tires of Shirnade's ATV. The machine roared, careened, and slipped wildly down the next steep slope.

Shirnade was thrown clear, and the big ATV bounced past him in a stroke of luck. He hit the sand running, stunned but coherent.

Marc cut the throttle and the auto-power disconnect, and leapt from the mighty ATV. He landed on Shirnade and tackled him. They hit and rolled down, down, down, until they landed at the bottom of the dune in a wide windswept ravine.

Shirnade managed to get to his feet but stumbled when he sank in the sand to his knees. He threw a wild left, and Marc ducked. He tried to free his feet for a kick, but Marc grabbed the free leg and twisted.

Shirnade screamed.

Marc hit with a right to the face, then a left to the solar plexus. The big Middle Easterner lost his breath and fell back.

Marc was on top of him, hitting with a hard right-left combination.

Shirnade rolled over and over in the sand to escape the onslaught.

Marc caught him hard in the face.

Shirnade managed to stumble to his feet. He came out of the sand and tried to strike Marc's chest with his left foot.

Marc blocked it and threw a kick to Shirnade's right kneecap. The man fell back and screamed in pain.

Marc stood over him and smiled. "Hurts like hell, don't it?"

Shirnade grimaced from the pain but managed to move again. He swiveled to his feet and fumbled for his weapon, but it had been lost in the crash. He tried to find the big knife, but it had shifted on his belt, and his hand couldn't locate it. He came around instead with a futile left hook.

Marc blocked it and slammed another foot into Shirnade's kneecap. He lost his balance for good this time as bones popped and a pain-filled scream echoed throughout the ravine.

Finally, Shirnade found the knife. He slashed at Marc's legs, the blade slicing only air.

Marc stumbled back, and his hand wrapped around the grip of his mighty Grizzly .45 Winchester Magnum. He came out with the massive weapon and leveled it on Shirnade's face. "Okay, dipshit, what'll it be? Drop the knife and go to prison, or keep the knife and go to hell?"

Shirnade froze. His hand cradled the knife, and he calculated the distance to Marc. He remained frozen for what seemed like hours, only seconds. His eyes glared fire, but his steel nerves kept his knife hand steady. He stared into Marc's eyes and said with a cold voice, "Can you look a man in the eyes and kill him?"

Marc's face was stone-cold. "Move that knife one inch, and you'll be dead before you know."

"Who are you, iceman?" Shirnade asked.

"Your doom," Marc said through clenched teeth.

"You're bluffing," Shirnade said confidently.

"This is a forty-five Winchester Magnum, and when it's finished with your face, you won't have one. If I'm bluffing, call it."

Shirnade lunged, the knife slashing out in a sweeping arch that found air, ended in sand, and cost him his life.

The mighty Grizzly roared, the massive slug caught Shirnade on the bridge of the nose, and a sea of blood sprayed into the air. When Shirnade's lifeless body crashed into the dune, the entire back of his head was scattered over the wet, red sand.

Carl was now more than a mile from where the melee had started, but Starr showed no signs of letting up. He ran the four-wheel ATV all out.

Carl laid a trail of autofire between the two ATVs. He purposely tried to keep from hitting the madman on the fleeing machine. Then Carl heard gunfire behind him. He glanced over his shoulder and saw two men on ATVs closing on him fast. Both had automatic weapons hurling thunder and lightning across the handlebars of their ATVs.

Bowman and Warner.

Carl steered a zigzag pattern and continued the pursuit. Hard-copper death rounds chewed sand and sent a sea of misty spray sailing in the wake of Carl's machine. He glanced back once more. The ATVs weren't gaining, but they still continued to chase him, autoguns blazing.

Carl checked the optical sight and leveled the rear-mounted Stinger miniguns on the center of the two men, between the ATVs. He tapped the firing switch, and lines of 5.56mm copper-jacketed death belched from the bores of the miniguns. Carl moved the optic sight in a figure eight and swept the area behind him. When the death dance was done, Bowman and Warner had crashed from their vehicles into the wet sand to pay the fiddler for a lifetime of dirty dancing.

Ahead now, Starr had found cover and was lying in wait to ambush his pursuer. He cut into a washout created by crashing waves from Lake Michigan and heavy rains. He jumped off the ATV and lifted the Uzi submachine gun from beneath his jacket. His wounded arm throbbed, but he steadied his aim toward Carl's ATV and unleashed a burst of full-auto fire.

The barrage missed. Carl cut the ATV to the right and headed up the steep slope of the dune. Machine-gun fire strafed the ground around him, pelting into the sand harmlessly.

Starr lost sight of his pursuer, but stayed poised behind the ATV and watched for the big black man on the ATV to reappear.

Carl worked his way over the top of the first small dune near the shore, then left the high-tech ATV and moved on foot, on the backside of the sandpile away from Lake Michigan's waters and parallel to the shore. He knew the guy with the gun was less than a hundred yards in front of him now. When he was almost even with where he thought Starr would be, he slipped to the top of the small dune and peered over.

He saw him. Starr was crouched down behind the ATV, holding the muzzle of his AK toward where he had last seen Carl's ATV. Carl moved slowly, the wind to his face, and eased the silenced 9mm Uzi from beneath his windbreaker jacket. Twenty feet from Andy Starr, he paused and then yelled, "You waiting on me, asshole?"

Starr spun around, startled. The AK-47 fully automatic rifle in his hands breathed fire as he jerked the muzzle around in a sweeping arc.

He was much too slow. Carl held the Uzi at his hip and unsheathed 9mm death from its thirty-two round magazine. The burst caught Starr in the chest, rose slightly, and zippered his upper body with permanent justice.

Starr fell backward, limp. The AK had fallen from his hands and lay in the sand beside him. Carl moved forward, the Uzi trained on the latest criminal scoured from the earth by cleansing hellfire. When he reached the body, he kicked the AK out of reach of Starr's still hands. He moved carefully, rolled the guy over, and inspected his wounds to be sure he was finished. He was. His neck and throat were chewed away by 147-grain hollow-point 9mm piranhas.

Carl threw the AK into the cold waters of Lake Michigan and ran hard for his ATV.

Rick Hosfelt streaked across the dunes in the pickup truck. He saw his chance to escape and took it. He continuously checked the rearview mirror to see if anyone was chasing him but saw no one. He was a half mile from the entrance to the winding sandy road that led into and out of the state park. He would, he decided, double back and make the run along the shoreline, then hit the trails used by the private tour company to make his escape. From there, he could make it to the main roads away from the killing fields. With the attaché case with five million dollars in cash and the PND that had been used as a sample, if he could just escape the dunes, he could disappear for a long, long time.

Hosfelt rolled the pickup across the top of a dune and went airborne down the backside. He straightened the machine, hit the accelerator hard, coasted to the bottom, then floored the gas pedal again to ascend the other side. When he checked the rearview mirror this time, he saw another pickup with three men in it. One drove, and two rode in the back. He could see weapons in the hands of the men in the bed and knew they were coming after him.

A hailstorm of gunfire streaked across the sands and slammed harmlessly into the bed of his truck. Hosfelt shifted into another gear and floored the gas once more. He climbed to the top of the dune and sailed over the crest.

He glanced into the mirror again and saw the two strange-looking ATVs closing in on the truck behind him.

He rolled down the backside of the dune and drove like a madman.

Marc looked right and saw Carl closing on the men in the pickup. He and Carl came in on the truck from opposite sides at forty-five degree angles.

The shooters, remnants of Shirnade's backup team, spotted Marc and Carl. They opened fire with a hailstorm of sizzling death pellets from the bed of the truck, but the violent motion of the truck caused the shots to sail harmlessly across the sand.

"Microrockèt on my mark, bro," Marc said into the VOX headset.

"Sighting and ready," said Carl. "Give the count."

The ATVs sped across the dunes while the shooters fired from the back of the truck. The driver seemed oblivious to anything but his pursuit of Rick Hosfelt in the truck in front of him.

"One. Two. Three. Fire!" Marc yelled. He pressed the firing switch on the handlebars, and a cloud of white smoke whooshed ahead of his speeding ATV.

Carl did the same thing. A loud *whoosh*, and a cloud of smoke streaked from his ATV also.

The impacts came almost in unison. Marc's microrocket slapped into the back of the speeding pickup, followed a microinstant later by the rocket from Carl's pod. A roaring explosion sent sand and debris upward in a fiery black cloud that sailed high, then rained back on the golden surface of the dunes. All three of Shirnade's men were obliterated before they knew what hit them.

"One to go," Carl quipped.

"Let's take him down," Marc replied.

The Highway Warriors throttled out their ATVs. The machines ran hard and fast, hitting dunes, sailing through the air, then landing again as they closed the gap on Rick Hosfelt. It took a minute and a half, but the mighty custom

ATVs ate the sand and distance with ease. They were within seventy-five yards of the fleeing pickup when the truck hit a high dune, bounced, and the PND sailed from the bed in the back onto the sandy surface of the dune.

"Let's take him," Carl yelled.

"Done," Marc replied. "Do it now."

Another streak of white smoke carved a trail across the sand that ended in a fireball when simultaneous rockets slapped into Hosfelt's fleeing ride. The truck, Rick Hosfelt, and five million dollars in cash went skyward in a cyclone of fire. In seconds, burning cash floated down to the dunes and was swept away on the wind to be buried forever by shifting sand.

Both Caroline Capenski and Jill Lanier had heard the explosions, but neither was fazed by them. Caroline sat idle, her autogun aimed at Jill in a foolish standoff. Her indecisiveness cost her precious seconds. She decided to try to outrun the Jeep and spun out amid a sea of sand across the dunes.

Jill gave chase. She stayed close, the bumper of her Jeep just feet from the rear end of Caroline's ATV, ready to dump hellfire into the wildly fleeing machine, but decided she would rather take the woman alive if possible.

Caroline's ATV cleared the top of a dune and sailed through the air, then hit loose sand and careened toward the bottom. When she looked up, she saw Marc's and Carl's ATVs top the dune in front of her. She spun sideways and twisted the machine around until it was headed straight back up the dune she had just jumped. She cut hard right and avoided Jill in the speeding Jeep Cherokee. The she throttled the ATV for all she could get and snaked up the dune.

Jill reached the bottom, cut hard, and made a 180-

degree skidding turn. She floored the Jeep's accelerator and headed back up the sandy hill in hot pursuit.

Caroline hit the top of the dune, sailed airborne over the rim, and hit the loose sand at an awkward angle. The ATV careened, skidded, and rolled over with a thunderous impact, throwing Caroline into the sand and narrowly missing her as it tumbled. She regained her senses and jumped to her feet, but not in time. Jill was already sliding to a stop. In a second, Jill was out and running toward Caroline. She tackled her in the sand.

Caroline go to her feet and threw a sweeping side kick. It missed. Jill came around with a pivoting roundhouse. Her foot caught Caroline in the face and sent her reeling. Almost before Caroline hit the sand, Jill was on top of her.

She drew the Beretta 92-F from its waist holster and pressed the barrel against Caroline's forehead. Her delicate voice became hard and mean as she spoke between clenched teeth. "Blink those cute little eyes the wrong way, and I'll splatter your brains all over this sandpile."

Caroline froze, her knees bent upward as she lay on her back in the sand. She stared into Jill's blue eyes and saw their fire. At that moment, she knew she had no choice. In a sweeping movement, she raked her left arm across the front of the gun and with her right pulled a boot knife out of a sheath on her right leg. She swung hard with the knife and tried to slash Jill's midsection, but Jill regained control of the Beretta. A double tap of death rang out as fire spat from the bore of the Beretta. Two hot missiles of death chewed through Caroline's face and sent her lifeless body prone on the sand in a torrent of blood.

Jill looked for a moment at the corpse, and for an instant a wave of nausea flowed over her. Then it passed. "I told you I never missed," she said, and she felt the coldness inside. She turned away. She looked across the dunes at the beauty polluted by scum. Marc and Carl approached from the top of a nearby dune, their ATVs running all out at the sound of gunfire. As she stood beside Caroline's body and watched them come toward her, she understood what Marc had told her more times that she cared to remember: *Killing never gets easier—but you do what you have to do. And always remember, we didn't start this madness, but we will do whatever we can to stop it. Permanently.*

ACTION ON EIGHTEEN WHEELS!

Here's a special preview of Book #11
in the OVERLOAD series

ALABAMA
BLOODBATH
by
Bob Ham

A cold-blooded druglord rules the Alabama un-
derworld with an iron fist. It's up to the Highway
Warriors to infiltrate the bloodthirsty ring and
break his grip from the inside . . . before the
body count gets much higher!

Look for OVERLOAD
wherever Bantam Books are sold.

The most important thing to Rick Baxter now was his ears—the ones on his head and the one taped right up the middle of his butt and attached to the tiny microphone pressed against the inside of his pants crotch. The micro-miniature FM body transmitter was tuned to 174.945 megaHertz and digitally encrypted to prevent unauthorized reception, which could prove fatal if it happened at the wrong time. The effective range of the transmitter was a half mile, and the signal quality was exceptional. The microphone was sensitive enough to detect the sound of a pencil falling on the floor across the room, yet the noise-canceling circuitry prevented interference from Baxter's movements. Without the ears, should something go sour, Baxter knew he was one dead narc. Fish bait.

Although it was after midnight, it was still business as usual at Bubba Ray Miles's waterfront "office." Tonight would mark the thirteenth buy in less than three weeks. It would also be the last. The long-awaited drug shipment had arrived earlier in the night by truck from somewhere up north. Baxter suspected Detroit. He was convinced of it, but he didn't have enough evidence to prove it in a court of law. When the packages were finished and the dealers came in off the street to get the next day's supply, all hell was gonna break loose. Hopefully, long before the goods could enter Bubba Ray's pipeline of eighteen-wheelers to be dispersed to his retailers around the country. The ear in Baxter's crotch heard everything. It had for several weeks now, and it sent it all to the Ampex multitrack tape recorder in the DEA van on the street a block away.

Then there was a knock at the door, and Rick Baxter felt his heart rate skyrocket.

Party time.

At Bubba Ray's command, McNally worked the locks and opened the door. Herschel Pope stood there, and with him another man who appeared unusually nervous.

Pope came inside, followed by his friend. "Bubba, this is Billy Dwayne Filbert. He's one of my runners down toward I-ten. Billy just got in off a *vacation* with Uncle Sam. Did three years of a ten-year rap. He's cool, and I asked him to help me move the goods tonight. Ain't no problem, is it?"

Rick Baxter tried to turn away casually. He recognized the face even before he heard the name. And it all crashed through his mind like a rampaging bull. Billy Dwayne Filbert. Memphis, Tennessee. Three and a half years ago. He had busted the guy, held him on the floor after a serious struggle, and almost dropped the hammer on him with his pistol stuck against his nose.

Baxter played it cool, but his stomach was churning. After all, back then there had been no beard, and his hair had been much shorter. But his features were still the same. There wasn't much he could do about that. Baxter held his breath and hoped the long hair and beard would be enough. He hoped—prayed—the druggie wouldn't recognize him.

Filbert looked around the room nervously. His eyes bored through Baxter. He stared for a moment before he spoke. "Hey, dude, don't I know you from somewhere?"

Baxter cringed but kept his cool. He stood from his chair and moved slowly toward the table. He looked at Bubba Ray, then at Filbert. He caught a glimpse of McNally across the room, and Richardson, poised with the Remington shotgun, ready to pump twelve-gauge death. Finally, his eyes settled back on Bubba Ray. "Boys, I been called a lot of things in my day, but never a narc. You better have something up your sleeve that I don't know about before you start callin' me a narc."

Bubba Ray's face was flushed red. He stared into Pope's eyes, and his lips tightened. "Damn you, Pope. You've ruined mah pardy."

"What?" Pope said.

"I know who Baxter is. Always *have* known. The joke's on him." Bubba Ray snapped his fingers, and the room was instantly a den of chaos. Gun-toting hardcases came through every entrance from every direction.

Rick Baxter held his breath as the cold steel muzzle of a pistol pressed against his temple. This was the big one. It might also be the last one if he didn't talk very fast and very, very convincingly.

In the van, Buddy Nichols was screaming into the microphone. "All units. Move now! It's a hard takedown. They've made Baxter. Take the place down now!"

Almost immediately, the continuous sound of gunfire rocked the silence of the night and masked the rhythm of the waves slapping into the drydocks. The docks erupted into a hellground of gunfire. The sound of a powerful boat engine roared over the automatic gunfire as it sped into Mobile Bay and headed for open water. But then a *whoosh* streaked across the night sky, leaving a trail of burning propellant as a DEA rocket sought and found the power boat. A thunderous explosion roared, and fiery debris flew into the sky, then rained back into the water.

Charlie Drake's hand wrapped around the pistol grip of a riot shotgun. He was out of his seat and heading for the door almost before Nichols finished the radio transmission. He opened the door and found himself looking into the shovel of a giant front-end loader that had materialized from the darkness. He fired a wasted shot of double-ought buckshot into the heavy steel shovel just an instant before the huge scoop slipped beneath the van and lifted it several feet into the air. Drake scrambled for the front of the van and another door.

Nichols lost his balance and slammed into the wall behind him with a brutal impact that dazed him for a moment. When he tried to regain his senses, a mountain of electronic equipment came down on top of him from the console and pinned him against the van's wall.

The front-end loader bounced across the pavement until it reached the dock while Drake struggled to get the door open on the driver's side. He managed to shove it up and open, found a solid footing against the steering wheel, and tried to get through the door. When he was almost free, he felt the van falling. He hit the cold ocean water first, followed a microinstant later by the van on top of him. Almost before he realized what had happened, he sank into the depths of Mobile Bay beneath three thousand pounds of high-tech surveillance van and equipment.

Back inside the dingy office, there was total chaos. At the first sound of gunfire, McNally had switched off the interior lights. People scrambled everywhere.

Rick Baxter hit the guy who held the gun at his head and knocked the weapon free. He spun to his right, shoving bodies out of his way in the darkness. Then he made a mad flying jump for the spot where he thought the dirty pane-glass window would be.

It was there. He hit it broad-shouldered and crashed through. He felt jagged edges of dirty glass slice into his flesh as he crashed onto the dock outside the office. He landed on his side in a roll and spun around to get to his feet. In the process, his bloody right hand went beneath his jacket and came out with a Sig 9mm automatic pistol. Baxter took three or four steps toward the safety of a large stack of cartons on the dock, but then his chest became a blazing inferno as a full load of double-ought buckshot tore through his flesh. He lost his balance as the pain screamed from every nerve in his body and slammed into his brain at the speed of light. He fell to the dock and lost his grip on the Sig. In the darkness, he realized he wasn't burning anymore. He was cold. Much colder than he should have been. But now there wasn't any pain, no feeling at all. Anywhere. His chest rocked, palpitated, and tried to get air, but there was none. It didn't matter anyway. When his eyes closed against a crashing sea of strange darkness and light, there was nothing except peaceful silence.

All three SCAT units, each from a different direction, hit the office at almost the same time. Streaks of blazing hellfire scorched through the dark night as automatic weaponfire sent death into the air. They entered Miles's office and found only darkness. Once they cleared the doors, more gunfire rattled and shook the walls.

The Mobile PD vice units hit the dock and surrounded the building. Then the darkness erupted into a sizzling hell. Gunfire came from everywhere. Shooters materialized from behind crates, out of darkened doorways, and from a line of eighteen-wheelers parked on the dock.

The SCAT units moved from the empty office and found themselves facing a wall of lead hornets that tore through the night. They retreated back into the office, but there was no sufficient cover. Shooters were everywhere, and death came from all directions at once. They fell back farther along the dock, but another wall of hellfire confronted them.

The vice units were caught in the death trap before they could react. Miles's shooters came at them with lethal ferocity. Two vice officers were trapped behind a stack of fiber bales in the front room nearest the street. They fired hard, selecting their targets and conserving ammunition. Then a dozen armed men moved toward them, gun barrels belching death and fire. When the officers tried to run for their lives, a barrage of lead death swept them from their feet and sent them into eternity.

The SCAT units were fighting hard. SCAT One screamed for reinforcements over the tactical radio headset, but his call to Nichols in the van went unanswered. The feds and vice units were outnumbered three to one as the battle raged.

Both men of SCAT Two found cover and engaged a half-dozen men from Miles's street-thug army in a heavy firefight. Two thugs were picked off by SCAT weapons, but the other four charged with total disregard for their lives. When the SCAT units scrambled for a safe retreat, a hand grenade slammed into the concrete dock and exploded. Both SCAT men flew, airborne, over the edge of the dock. Their bodies were ripped and torn before they hit the surface of the bay. Then they disappeared beneath the rolling water.

At the first hint of trouble, Bubba Ray Miles had moved through the side door leading into another dark warehouse section of the drydock building. He left Filbert and Pope to the mercy of the feds. Ronnie Richardson was the point man, leading Bubba Ray and McNally through the maze of crates and cartons stacked in the dark building. They took cover there and waited for the shooting to stop. When it didn't, Bubba Ray decided to escape without waiting for the end of his "pardy."

"Ronnie, we can take the catwalk across the top of the building and get to them trucks parked at the end of the building. You go first and knock off any of them federal boys totin' guns out there," Bubba Ray whispered. "Mah boys can take care of anybody left nosin' 'round down heah. I don't want a single one of them po-leese left standin'."

Richardson nodded and moved out, climbing the ladder ahead of Bubba Ray. McNally took the rear and watched for trouble behind them. They reached the cat-walk and moved across the top of the building. Then the gunfire came. A Mobile vice officer opened fire from behind an air-conditioning unit atop the roof. Richardson turned fast and dumped a barrage of death from the Ingram MAC-10. The cop fell over and lay kicking on the rooftop.

"Gimmie that greasegun, Ronnie," Bubba Ray said.

"What you gonna do, boss?" Richardson asked.

"I b'lieve that-un's still alive. I be right back," Bubba Ray said. He moved from his protective prone position and went cautiously toward the fallen lawman. When he got there, he could see the look of fear and pain etched across the man's face, illuminated by the dock lights. "Howdy," he said as he kicked his gun out of his reach.

The wounded officer looked into Bubba Ray's eyes and glanced at the muzzle of the Ingram pointed at his face. "Miles, you're crazy. You can't kill cops and get away with it. They'll hang you for this. Somebody will find you."

Bubba Ray laughed and bit down on the stub of his cigar. "Hell, boy, I been hung like a mule since the day I was born," he said, and he laughed louder. "As far as gettin' away with anythin', ain't nobody left alive that saw me. I never was heah. You boys ought to learn to mind your own business and leave us workin' folks alone. I'm gonna kill you now."

The cop's face tightened as he clenched his teeth. Then the Ingram barked a staccato burst of .45-caliber Hydra-Shoks, and the cop's muscles went limp.

Bubba Ray looked up into the night sky at the full moon and smiled. Then he turned his attention back to the dead cop, and he chewed the end of his cigar. "I tole you, weren't nobody left alive that saw me heah. Nobody."

The drive from Dallas to Mobile had been a leisurely one. Carl Browne drove most of the way, while Marc Lee rode shotgun in the passenger seat. Jill Lanier relaxed in the sleeper of the comfortable cab and kept her head poked through the curtains to carry on a conversation while the miles clicked by with vanishing white lines.

When they reached Mobile, they drove over the bay on I-65 and checked out the area where the USS *Alabama* lay anchored. They decided to drive one of the Jeep Cherokees stored in the trailer rather than attempt to weave the rig through the maze of the parking area designated for tours of the old warship. They found a truck stop at I-10 and I-65, and parked the Leeco rig there. Then they off-loaded the red Cherokee and secured the rig. Marc drove east until they reached the exit that would take them to the *Alabama*. When they finally reached the parking lot, it was vacant except for two light-colored sedans. Marc glanced at his watch and saw it was 8:45.

"We're early, but I guess that won't matter," he said as he parked as close to the entrance to the warship-turned-tourist-attraction as he could get.

"I see the welcoming committee," Carl said as the Jeep's headlights fell upon two men in business suits who stood near the ship's entrance ramp. "Two of the FBI's finest."

"I wonder why he wanted to meet here?" said Jill.

"Security would be my guess," Marc replied. "How much safer can you get than a vacant ship docked in a bay? The tourists are long gone for the day. They probably have the run of the place. Besides, I kind of like the idea. An old battlewagon sounds like as good a place as any to start a new battle, huh?"

Jill laughed. "Yeah," she said. "An old warship and a brand-new battle in another old war. Appropriate, I suppose."

Jill, Marc, and Carl left the Jeep and walked toward the ramp. The two men in business suits met them halfway.

Before the Highway Warriors could speak, one of the men said, "Colonel Lee, Major Browne, Ms. Lanier, I'm Special Agent Donald Crossfield, and this is Special Agent Tim Barnes. Glad to see you here."

"Gentlemen, nice to meet you," Marc said.

"Same here," Carl replied.

"Yeah, me too," said Jill.

Crossfield shook hands with the Warriors, then Barnes did the same. Crossfield turned and gestured toward the ship. "If you folks would be kind enough to follow me, Agents Harrison and Crain are waiting for you in the captain's quarters. The ship is empty except for us, so you needn't be concerned with security."

"She certainly is a stately old tub," Carl said as they walked up the gangway.

"Yes, she is," said Barnes. "She saw a lot of action in her time. She's a thirty-five-thousand-long-ton battleship. Her prime was during World War Two. When the navy decided to take her out of service and put her in mothballs in the early nineteen-sixties, the people of Mobile, all of Alabama in fact, raised money to restore her and make her what she is today. People come from all parts of the country just to stand on her decks and daydream about her glory days."

"Nice," Marc said as he looked to her top deck at the rotating gun turrets. "How long have Crain and Harrison been here?"

"About an hour," Crossfield said. "After the boat closed for the day, we swept it, and then they boarded. They have slides and some videotape footage for you. Strikes me as unusual, though—why are military people like you guys called in on something like this?"

"Well," Marc said, "I'm not sure what *this* is. We're following instructions. That's all I can tell you. When the Boss barks, we listen."

"Yeah, a lot of that going around," Crossfield quipped. He exited the top of the gangway and stepped onto the main deck of the historic old battleship.

Marc, Carl, and Jill followed. Barnes brought up the rear and checked behind himself to be sure there was no one else in the parking lot or near the ship.

"This way," Crossfield said. He led the Warriors across the deck until they reached a small door near the tower. He opened it and stepped inside. A narrow steep stairway led down to the lower deck. Dim but adequate lights glowed along the way. Movement was slow and footing uncertain as the entourage made their way belowdecks.

When they reached the lower deck, they moved along a narrow hallway through open watertight airlock doors until they reached the doorway marked CAPTAIN'S QUARTERS. Crossfield knocked on the door, then opened it.

He stepped inside and gestured for the Warriors to follow him.

Two men sat across the small room reviewing files and maps. When the door opened, both of them looked up.

Brittin Crain spoke first. "Hi, guys, it's been a while. Come on over and find yourselves a chair. I apologize for the accommodations, but under the circumstances, I felt this would be the place that would best suit our needs."

"Still findin' time for the weight room, I see," Marc said. "You look like a gorilla in a business suit, Brittin."

Crain laughed.

"Don't listen to him, Brittin," Jill said. "You still look great."

"Carl," said Crain and extended his hand. "How goes it, brother?"

"Still hangin' in there, Brittin, but we all have our days," Carl said as he accepted Crain's hand.

Special-Agent-in-Charge Harvey Harrison exchanged

greetings, then looked at Barnes and Crossfield. "Position at each end of the hallway. We don't want to be disturbed unless this tub is under attack or sinking. No one comes in. Period."

"Yes, sir," Crossfield said. "We'll take care of it."

Everyone sat down, and Brittin Crain opened a file folder. Inside was a photograph of a man—young, late twenties or early thirties. Crain flipped it on the table where everyone could see it. "That's Special Agent Rick Baxter of the DEA. He died two nights ago right across the bay from here. He was murdered, along with thirteen of his companions. They were shot down in cold blood during a planned raid on a major drug-distribution location. From all appearances, the hit team for the bust was set up in a big way. Once they were inside, they were hit from front and back. A crack federal SCAT unit was completely mowed down. Seven dead feds and seven from Mobile PD vice. Two street thugs were gunned down. A man named Pope, Herschel James, and another named Filbert, Billy Dwayne. They were after this man—Miles, Bubba Ray. He's the major source in these parts for all sorts of illegal substances. Former moonshiner and a permanent go-to-hell attitude. I have a complete file on him and several of his accomplices. To make a very long story very short, the Boss wants you to find Bubba Ray and terminate his empire. No one can prove he was involved, at least not yet, but we're spending hundreds of man-hours on his case as we speak. We can't prove it in a court of law, but it's proven to the satisfaction of the Boss. His instructions are to topple the kingdom and end the king's reign. In the process, find the leak inside Mobile PD, the DEA, wherever it is, and plug it. Permanently."

No one spoke, but shocked blank faces stared at one another.

Marc stared at the file and the photographs. "Bubba

Ray seems to be a mean man. Is he as vicious as this would indicate, or has he just built himself a reputation?"

"Oh, he's mean, all right. He'd kill his mother if he thought he could make a buck on the deal," Harrison said. "He's a primo hardcase in the first degree."

"Is he smart enough to pull off something this incredible without getting caught?" Carl asked.

"Apparently," Crain said. "He's still a free man. There is nothing—repeat, nothing—left of physical evidence that would place Miles at the scene of the murders. But the other side to the guy is frightening. What he lacks in education, he makes up in guts. He fears nothing."

"Get in on the inside," Harrison said. "Get on Bubba Ray's good-ole-boy roster, then pull his plug and bring him down. You'll have the support you need, but I must warn you, this man is a cold-blooded killer who does it because he likes it. All of his pawns are puppets. He pulls the strings, and they dance. They'll cut your throats and feed your guts to the fishes if you mess up. It's a one-shot deal. Study the portfolios, the slides, and the videotape. Move at your leisure. Just one hitch."

"And that is?" Marc asked.

Harrison sat stone-faced. He glanced up from the folders and stared at the Warriors. "The Boss wants it wrapped up with ribbons on it within two weeks."

Action on Eighteen Wheels!

Marc Lee and Carl Browne, ex-Delta Force anti-terrorist commandos: They've taken on bloodthirsty Middle Eastern terrorists...deadly drug cartels...vicious bikers...the Mafia...no matter how badly they're outnumbered, Lee and Browne always come up swinging...and blasting!

Don't miss any of the exciting books in Bob Ham's OVERLOAD SERIES!